SHARON KENDRICK

Kiss and Tell

REVENGE
is Sweet

D0049644

Harlequin Books

TORONTO • NEW YORK • LONDON
AMSTERDAM • PARIS • SYDNEY • HAMBURG
STOCKHOLM • ATHENS • TOKYO • MILAN
MADRID • WARSAW • BUDAPEST • AUCKLAND

ISBN 0-373-11951-8

KISS AND TELL

First North American Publication 1998.

Copyright © 1997 by Sharon Kendrick.

Printed in U.S.A.

Three houses, three couples—three reasons for revenge

The calm surface of life in St. Fiacre's Hill— where lavish homes provide a secure haven for the seriously rich—hides a maelstrom of feeling. Geraint Howell-Williams, Triss Alexander and Dominic Dashwood all think they have a need to avenge—but the actions each sets in motion gain a life of their own, with entirely unexpected results.

Kiss and Tell is the second book in Sharon Kendrick's REVENGE IS SWEET trilogy. Look out for Dominic's story in *Settling the Score* (#1957), coming next month.

Dear Reader,

"Revenge is a dish best served cold."

The above line grabbed my attention the very first time I read it. Revenge is a strong, deep emotion—passion with a dark, sometimes bitter side to it—and I have chosen it as the linking theme for my St. Fiacre's books.

I like the idea of my characters—all outwardly highly successful people—having a secret side to their natures. A side that can plot to avenge themselves, a side that might sometimes appall them, but that they are powerless to resist—for the darkest emotions are always the most irresistible....

What motivates revenge? It is always the sense of having been wronged, a chance to win after an earlier defeat. And like all deep, controlling passions, revenge has a cumulative effect.

But don't take my word for it—find out yourself from Geraint, Triss and Dominic....

Sharon Kendrick

CHAPTER ONE

WOULD he come? That was the question. A question which could only be answered by the man himself, all six feet four of him, with his unruly hair and his Irish eyes and that irreverent humour which always seemed to be lurking at the corners of a mouth just made for kissing.

Triss shivered. She must just be patient, and wait. She had waited fourteen months, after all, so another few minutes were neither here nor there.

In fact, what she *should* do was to make herself remember why she had split up with Cormack Casey in the first place.

And after that she should force herself to recall every single one of his bad points, so that a miracle might happen and she might remain immune to him.

Some hopes.

The sound of the waves beating down on the wet blond sand outside the cottage rang in her ears. Triss glanced down at her watch and for the twentieth time she wondered how Simon was. She had never been away from her beautiful blue-eyed baby before, and had been totally unprepared for the almost *physical* pain of his absence.

No one ever warned you what babies would *do* to you, she thought, with a sudden rush of overwhelming love. How motherhood would change you irrevocably, so that the person you used to be before you had the baby seemed like a distant stranger.

The cottage she had rented had been deliberately chosen for its lack of television and telephone. Cormack was a man whom other people clamoured to be with. When they had lived together his phone had never stopped ringing—hence the lack of facilities in this out-of-the-way place. But, even more importantly, she wanted *all* his attention when she dropped her bombshell into his lap.

She had given the number of the local pub to Lola—who was looking after Simon for her—with the instructions that she was to ring Triss immediately if there was *anything* she wasn't happy about.

Please God, there wouldn't be.

She thought of the comfort and security of her elegant house on the exclusive St Fiacre's Hill estate, bought with the earnings from her successful modelling career. The perfect place, she had decided during her pregnancy, in which to bring up her baby.

Triss swallowed down the ever-present fears which were part and parcel of motherhood and allowed herself a fleeting glance in the mirror, wincing slightly as she did so.

The simple rust-coloured linen dress she had chosen was practical and comfortable, but it made her look so *mumsy*—and today it seemed to drain all the colour from her skin.

Should she have worn make-up? she wondered.

She had decided against it in the end. Make-up might seem contrived, as though she was trying to focus all Cormack's attention on *her*, while nothing could be further from the truth.

Her face was pale—paper-pale—with the freckles which spattered her small snub nose standing out in stark relief. Her green and golden eyes were as big as beacons, but tiny lines of strain, fanning out from the corners, could be seen if you looked closely. Though she doubted that Cormack would be interested in looking closely.

At least she wasn't holding out any hope that Cormack would attempt to seek some form of reconciliation with her today. She looked a completely different person from the woman he had first met— with her red-brown hair all shorn off, her face completely bare of make-up. And hadn't Cormack loved the fact that her model-girl looks were so flamboyant that millions of men lusted after her?

Well, she couldn't imagine anyone lusting after her now...

She heard the distant sound of an engine, and her ears pricked up even as she frowned, trying to work out what made this particular engine sound quite unlike any car she had ever come across. But only one man in the world would drive to a beach in something which sounded like Concorde breaking through the sound barrier!

Cormack!

Triss ran her fingertips beneath her eyes, as if by doing so she could magically remove the dark smudges of so many sleepless nights. Then she bit down hard on her bottom lip so that the blood rushed in to give her mouth some colour.

And waited.

The cottage was right off the beaten track—that had been one of the main reasons for choosing it. The beach made it fairly inaccessible, and you had to park your car right at the top and then clamber down over a low wall before you could walk across the sand to the house.

So how come she could hear the engine getting closer and closer, its loud, buzzing intensity sounding like a giant insect gone mad?

Triss flung the front door open and saw the sleek black and silver machine which was noisily growling its way to a halt right in front of the cottage, sludging up the pale, hard sand as it did so.

Trust Cormack to hire himself a motorbike, she thought, torn between exasperation and admiration. It had been one of the things which had both attracted and infuriated her—the fact that Cormack Casey was like no other man in the world.

The man in question was now pulling off an outrageous silver and scarlet crash-helmet, and Triss held her breath to see whether he had adopted a more sober and sensible hairstyle which might better reflect his reputation as Hollywood's hottest, sharpest and hunkiest scriptwriter.

He hadn't!

And Triss was unprepared for the relief which flooded through her as she caught sight of that magnificent mane of dark hair which grew down the tanned column of his neck. Too long and too tousled, it gleamed blue-black beneath the pale light of the March sun, with its riotous waves looking as though some frantic woman had just run her fingers all the way through it.

Triss swallowed down the dark, bitter taste of jealousy and looked into eyes as deeply blue as the finest lapis lazuli. Simon's eyes, she thought suddenly, with the shock of recognition.

'Hello, Beatrice,' he said unsmilingly, and his voice sounded at once strange and yet poignantly familiar.

The Irish accent, she noted, was still intact, though now it held the faintest trace of a soft Mid-Atlantic twang. Hardly surprising, Triss supposed, seeing as how he had been living in the States since the age of sixteen.

'Hello, Cormack,' she said, her own voice sounding reedy and weak—but that was hardly surprising either. She had been unprepared for the impression he always made on her, and that was sheer stupidity. How on earth could she have forgotten just how devastating he was in the flesh?

He was dressed from head to toe in black leather. A leather jacket clung to shoulders as broad as a labourer's and then tapered down to the curved indentation of his waist, and below the jacket were leather jeans—black and outrageously snug, the soft material caressing the muscular definition of his thighs, and on and on down his seemingly endless legs.

Leather, thought Triss despairingly. That most sensual of fabrics, with its sleek look and slick feel and its exciting, animal scent.

Those intelligent blue eyes didn't miss a trick. He observed her gaze wandering, hypnotised, over every centimetre of his body. 'Like it?' he queried softly.

'What?' she whispered.

'The leather.' His eyes glittered. 'Some women find it a turn-on.'

'Is that why you wore it?'

'I'm not sure. Perhaps subconsciously?'

'You look like a labourer,' she said sweetly. 'Or a degenerate rock star.'

The first smile came then—a typically roguish Cormack-type smile—and Triss was unprepared for its impact. Stupidly unaware that the sight of it would set her heart racing as it had done so many times before. *Damn* him! she thought indignantly. He knows. He *knows* what that smile can do to a woman. And it's an unfair advantage!

'Well, that's appropriate, isn't it?' he drawled. 'As I've been both a labourer *and* a rock star. Though never degenerate.' There was a long pause while he studied her. 'You've had your hair cut, Triss,' he said eventually, and there was an odd note of surprise in his voice.

Triss had been holding her breath, waiting for all the comments he *could* have made, and felt oddly disappointed that Cormack, of all people, should have said something so commonplace.

For the first time she felt a glow of something approaching achievement—that she had had the strength to remove the trademark which had eventually trapped her. 'Yes,' she agreed evenly. 'All chopped off.'

'When?' he demanded, as though she were a suspect he was cross-examining.

This was a touch more difficult—she had had her thick red-brown hair shorn on the day she had discovered she was pregnant. It had seemed a very symbolic and necessary thing to do at the time. She gave a careless little shrug. 'Can't remember,' she lied.

The blue eyes narrowed disbelievingly. 'Really? Can you remember *why* you did it?'

Triss managed to return his hard, questioning stare. 'Why shouldn't I cut it? Models often change their image—'

'But you don't model any more, do you, Triss?'

Her eyes widened. How much, she wondered anxiously, did he already know? 'Wh-what do you mean?'

He frowned. 'Good God, woman—has your brain gone to mush, or are my questions so complex that I'm going to have to clarify each and every one?'

'There's no need to be so sarcastic!' Triss shot back furiously, remembering how his razor-sharp mind had always been able to make her feel so ridiculously inferior. But no more. No more. '*Is* there?'

'No.' He gave her a steady look. 'OK, I *presume* that you've given up modelling—mainly because I never see you in any of the glossies these days. And you certainly aren't very visible on the catwalk. Are you?'

Had he perhaps been following her career? Hope stirred foolishly in her heart, but Triss firmly repressed it. 'No. That's right. I'm not modelling these days.'

Arrogant black brows which looked as though an artist had swept them on darkly and indelibly against that high, intelligent forehead curved upwards in bemused question. 'And why's that? You were the best model of your generation.'

Trust Cormack, thought Triss in some alarm. He had always had the knack of getting to the point without any effort whatsoever. Give him a couple more minutes and he would have extracted her reason for inviting him here, and that was not her plan at all!

She did not intend to blurt anything out. Not now—not on the doorstep with a bitter March wind blowing up a storm around them.

She had planned it out so carefully in her mind. They were supposed to have a civilised period chatting together. A reacquaintance over the simple lunch she had prepared. Something calm and unemotional which befitted modern, enlightened ex-lovers who knew all the rules of the dating game. Before she dropped her bombshell.

'Why don't we go inside?' she suggested quickly. 'It's warmer in there. The kettle is on the boil, and I'm making some soup.' She cast up her eyes expressively at the oyster-grey sky. 'It looks like soup kind of weather, doesn't it?'

'It sure does.' His mouth moved in a sardonic twist, and he said nothing more as he followed her inside, but Triss could guess what he was thinking.

In the days when they had lived together Triss had scarcely known one end of a kettle from another. And their relationship had never progressed beyond the tempestuous passion stage to the living in relative harmony stage.

How people changed, she reflected as Cormack walked into the sitting room, shutting the front door behind him. Well, *she* had certainly changed—she had had to—but had Cormack?

'You've lit a fire,' he observed in surprise as he placed his helmet on the floor beside one of the armchairs and began to unzip his black leather jacket.

'Yes.' For the first time, humour danced in her hazel eyes.

'And what's so funny?' he murmured casually, though his blue eyes were very watchful.

'You,' she answered without thinking. 'Making all these conventional observations. It doesn't sound like you at all, Cormack.'

'And Triss Alexander lighting fires and boiling kettles and concocting soups—that doesn't sound like *you* at all, either. So what do you think that says about *us*, hmm?'

Triss shrugged. 'I'll leave all the deductions to you, I think,' she answered brightly. 'After all, that's what you're good at.'

'But I thought that *you* were the queen of jumping to conclusions,' he parried softly. 'After all, I only had to speak two words to a woman and everyone knew that I *must* be sleeping with her, didn't they, Triss?'

His caustic words brought back the aching and humiliating memories of sexual jealousy, and Triss felt all the remaining colour drain from her cheeks.

Was she setting herself up for more of the same? The same kind of limbo she'd used to live in constantly when she was with Cormack? She had hated the person she'd eventually become—with her checking and counter-checking and her suspicions about him. Her insane jealousy had appalled both her *and* him, and yet she had been powerless to change her behaviour.

She drew in a deep breath. She had not brought Cormack here today to resurrect old battles. She was a mother now, and a responsible grown-up woman of twenty-four. She must lead by example, and surely if she was calm and mature and remained unruffled, then Cormack might behave likewise? 'Are you hungry?' she asked politely.

The ironic twist of his mouth acknowledged her formality as he sank down into the armchair nearest the fire, his leather clothes making little swishing sounds as the fabric moved in conjunction with his big, muscular limbs. 'Starving,' he admitted. 'But I need a drink first.'

Triss was startled. She thought about the supplies she had brought with her. One bottle, and she wasn't even sure if there was a corkscrew in the place. 'I have wine,' she told him rather hesitantly. 'But that's all.'

'I meant tea, actually,' he said, with a disbelieving little look at the grandfather clock which ticked loudly in one corner of the over-furnished room. 'Goodness me, Triss,' he murmured admonishingly. 'Offering me alcohol before midday—what degenerate circles *you* must have been mixing in!'

If only he knew! 'I'll make a pot,' she said stiffly, and headed off into the kitchen where she welcomed the chance to busy herself with kettle and cups and saucers. The activity stopped her from thinking too much, and she willed her hands to stop trembling, but they steadfastly refused to obey her.

He had not moved when she carried the loaded tea-tray back in and the sight of him in that tiny, old-fashioned room, all brooding masculinity and black leather, conjured up the image of something both sensual and forbidden.

With his gleaming blue eyes and devil-may-care air, Cormack Casey looked the embodiment of the kind of man most mothers warned their daughters against.

Unless you happened to have a mother like hers, thought Triss bitterly, who fancied Casey rotten herself and had delighted in enlightening Triss as to what kind of man he really was.

'Here.' He had gracefully risen to his feet and was holding his hands out. 'Let me take that from you.'

Triss blushed, knowing that she was at her most vulnerable when he was gentle to her. 'It's OK, thank you. I can manage.'

'But it's heavy, sweetheart—here.' And he cap-
tured the tray from her with ease. 'Sit down,' he
instructed. 'And stop glowering at me like that.'

Glowering was her only defence against being
called 'sweetheart' in that irresistibly lilting Irish
way of his. She was trying all the while to tell herself
that the affectionate term meant nothing—nothing
at all. It was a phrase people used all the time in
Belfast.

She had heard him say it to just about everyone
in the past, particularly when he took a break from
working, when he was on a roll and in one of those
extravagantly happy moods which made women
who were total strangers thrust their phone numbers
into his pocket in restaurants.

At the time, Triss had pretended to laugh at his
entirely instinctive flirting—as he had laughed—but
his ability to laugh had hurt almost as much as his
refusal to rebuff the women who drooled all over
him.

'Does it turn you on,' she had demanded one
day, 'to have all these women fawning over you and
making themselves blatantly available?'

'You seem to forget that *I* have a say in all this,
Triss,' he had told her frowningly, with a shrug of
those massively broad shoulders. 'These women feel
they know me because they happen to have seen a
couple of my films. So am I to be rude to them in
public? It just makes it less confrontational if I let
them leave their pieces of paper and smile politely.
Later on, I bin them. I don't know why it bothers
you, sweetheart. It means nothing, and it has

nothing, absolutely *nothing* to do with you and me. Understand?'

So Triss had forced herself to nod bravely, while the memory of those telephone numbers had scorched into her heart like a blow-torch and she'd tortured herself with wondering whether he had actually thrown them *all* away.

Now he poured black tea into one of the delicate china cups the cottage had provided, and handed it to her.

She shook her head rather apologetically. 'I don't take it black any more, Cormack. I'll have milk and two sugars in it, please.'

He very nearly dropped the cup. '*What* did you say?'

She almost smiled. 'You heard.'

He nodded his head so that inky tendrils danced enticingly around his ears. 'Yes, I heard.' He dropped two lumps of sugar into the cup and added milk before returning it to her with those black brows of his arrogantly arched in query. 'So when did you give up the starvation diet?'

When she had discovered that running up and down stairs to tend to a crying baby beat any aerobics class for using up energy! She sipped at her tea gratefully and looked at him. 'I was never on a starvation diet, Cormack,' she objected. 'Just—'

'I know! I know!' He held his hand up and recited in a careless, bored tone, 'Just no chocolate for your skin, no alcohol for your early mornings, sugar made you sluggish—'

'It was my *career*!' Triss snapped back. 'And I wanted to do it to the best of my ability—which did not include staggering into an early shoot with a hangover, having survived on just three hours' sleep, because *you* wanted to go partying!'

Humour, which had stayed dormant in the depths of those lapis lazuli eyes, now shone through, nearly swamping her in its soft blue blaze. 'But I thought you *liked* partying,' he observed in that low, sexy drawl of his, rubbing his chin thoughtfully while he watched her.

'I suppose I did. At first.' Triss shook her head, wondering if she would ever get used to feeling her neck so exposed and vulnerable. She missed her long hair, that was the trouble, but cutting it off had come to symbolise the whole new way of life she had embraced. And if she grew it back again would she become that passive, prying clothes-horse she had grown to despise? 'But after a while it wore me down. And those parties bored me.'

'But you never actually said anything,' he remarked.

'No.' She had just withdrawn and sulked like a schoolgirl—expecting Cormack to be able to *guess* the reason for her discontent, feeling disappointed when he did not. And disappointed too, she had to admit, that she on her own was not enough for Cormack. That he liked, even needed those parties.

Cormack picked up his cup in the distinctive way which Triss remembered so well, cradling it between his palms, seeking warmth from it like a Scout sitting round a camp fire. 'We should have talked about it,' he observed. 'Maybe come to a compromise.'

Triss cocked him a glance. 'When?'

His eyes gleamed as he sipped his tea, the look on his face leaving her in no doubt as to what he was thinking about. 'I take your point,' he murmured. 'We didn't actually *do* a lot of talking, did we, Triss?'

To her fury, Triss found herself blushing. She had *meant* that both her and Cormack's heavy work schedules had conflicted, giving them very little free time with each other, but Cormack had obviously misinterpreted her meaning. Deliberately? she wondered. She lifted her chin. 'No,' she answered, sounding surprisingly cool. 'We didn't.'

His eyes glittered at her. 'Anyway, as I recall, Beatrice, you didn't find the parties *completely* boring. You enjoyed dressing up to the nines so that the whole room went silent as you walked in. Didn't you?' he finished softly.

'I needed to look my best, yes,' she argued defensively. 'Because I wanted to make sure that I had enough work. And my agent always told me to go out with the thought that people were going to judge me by my appearance. If you will remember, those were the days before it became acceptable for models to grunge around in public wearing their oldest clothes with their hair scraped back into an elastic band. And besides, you liked me to dress up, Cormack—don't deny that.'

'Yes, I did like it.' He nodded, his face reflective. 'Your beauty astonished me, if you must know. I was as dazzled as the rest of them. When you pulled out all the stops to really dress up, I could hardly believe that you were with *me*—the upstart from Belfast!'

'Like a trophy on your arm, you mean?' she challenged drily. 'Is that it?'

He shook his head so that the ebony waves gleamed as blackly as a raven's wing, but his blue eyes were cold—icy-cold, like a frozen sea. 'I'm not the kind of man who needs a beautiful woman to define him, Beatrice. You were there because I liked you—no other reason.'

And now? Triss swallowed, wondering when exactly they had stopped liking one another. She forced down another mouthful of tea, then looked directly into that strong, vibrant face which exuded so much earthy sensuality. 'You're still very laid-back, aren't you, Cormack?' she said.

'In what way?'

'Well, I would have thought that most men would have burst in here demanding to know just *why* they were here. Not sat there calmly drinking tea like a civilised stranger.'

'We're neither civilised, nor strangers. Not really—are we, Triss?' His eyes glittered with an unspoken message of remembered desire, and Triss had to fiercely blot out the memory of lying naked in Cormack's bed while he taught her everything he knew about the art of lovemaking.

And it had shocked as well as thrilled her to discover just how much he *did* know.

'As to what most men would do—well, that doesn't really concern me. All I know is that the woman I lived with, who disappeared so conclusively from my life after a night of the most spectacular sex I've ever experienced—'

Triss clapped her cool palms up to her flaming cheeks. 'Cormack, don't—'

'Don't what? Don't tell the truth?' he demanded. 'Why? Does it disturb you so much?' He smiled, but Triss could detect the anger which burned slowly behind the appearance of humour. 'Why should she then send me a message—quite out of the blue—asking me to meet her at some God-forsaken place on the southern coast of England?'

'Was it difficult to arrange?'

He shot her a narrow-eyed look. 'I've reached the stage in my career where very little is difficult to arrange.'

It suddenly occurred to her that she had simply expected him to drop everything and just come to her.

And he *had*! Hope sprang to life in her heart, like the first snowdrop after the austerity of winter. If she asked him, might he answer all her hopes and dreams and prayers and say that he had missed her? Triss took her courage in both hands and said, 'And why *did* you come so readily?'

He smiled. 'I'm intrigued as to why you asked me, if you must know, Triss. And the sensation of being intrigued these days is so rare that I feel honour-bound to savour every moment.'

Disappointment lanced through her, but somehow she managed to keep her features neutral. 'How jaded you sound, Cormack!' she observed critically. 'And how cynical!'

His eyes glittered like blue ice. 'That's the price you pay for success, sweetheart.'

'Are you after the sympathy vote?' she demanded. 'Because you won't get it from me, you know!'

'*I'm* not after anything,' he told her pointedly. 'You were the one who invited me here, so *you*, presumably, are the one who is after something. I'm still waiting for you to tell me what it is.'

'And you don't seem to be in any hurry to find out,' she observed in surprise, wondering why everything felt as though it was going horribly wrong.

'I'm a patient man.' He smiled, but the smile did not reach his eyes, and for the first time since she had decided to contact him Triss felt a whisper of fear skittering down the length of her spine.

'Are you?' she asked him in a low voice. 'You must have changed, then, Cormack.'

'We all change, Triss. It's inevitable—it's part of life and of growth. Without change, we stagnate and die.'

And suddenly it was more than just reluctance to tell him about Simon; it was fear.

For Cormack was fundamentally a man of morals—an honourable man.

Once, in a rare, confiding moment, he had told her that in the past he had fallen for the wife of one of his greatest friends—something which he had despised himself for doing. He had convinced himself that he had kept his affection secret, but the woman must have guessed—or maybe it had been what she had been praying for herself.

She had waited until her husband was away on a trip, and then had plotted her grand seduction. She had crept into Cormack's bed late one night, knowing he was at a party, and lain in wait for him in all her glorious golden nakedness.

Triss remembered the look of intense strain etched on his face as he had described how he had quietly asked the woman to leave.

'But wasn't it tempting—to let her stay?' Triss had asked him breathlessly.

Lying next to her in bed, looking so bronzed and so gorgeous, Cormack had given her a look which had made her feel terribly young and terribly naïve. 'Of course it was tempting,' he had answered quietly. 'The forbidden always is. But friendship rates highly in my book. Certainly above lust.'

'*Lust?*' she had queried, appalled. 'Not love?'

He had smiled coldly. 'How could it be love?' he asked her. 'To love someone you have to get to know them properly—and you certainly can't do that while they are married to someone else.'

Strange that she should remember that conversation now, thought Triss—especially after all this time. Was some self-protective instinct reminding her of just how ruthless and cold Cormack could be when he chose?

Triss had eyes which were sometimes green and sometimes gold—depending on the light, or how she happened to be feeling at the time. In her modelling days she had acquired the skill of being able to make her face reflect whichever mood the art director was searching for, but these days she was badly out of practice.

She let her heavy lids drop, like a demure Victorian heroine, for fear that Cormack's intelligent, searching eyes would guess at more than she wanted him to.

'So tell me, have *you* changed, sweetheart?' he queried in that lilting Irish accent which managed to be soft and sweet and hard and sexy all at the same time.

'I suppose I must have done,' answered Triss slowly, for she certainly could not have imagined taking motherhood so much in her stride when she was living with Cormack.

In fact, when she thought about it now, she had taken *nothing* in her stride when she'd lived with Cormack. But then she had been completely out of her depth. And, although she'd been earning a fortune from modelling when they had met, her fame had been small-beer when compared with the man who had been dubbed 'Hollywood's most eligible bachelor' by the trade papers as well as the tabloids.

Triss had always been scornful of such extravagant soubriquets, and it hadn't been until she'd met Cormack Casey that she'd realised that for once the papers had not exaggerated...

CHAPTER TWO

Triss first met Cormack in the most romantic city in the world.

She met him in Paris. In springtime.

In fact, Cormack told her much later that he would never have written it as it had actually happened—it was so corny that audiences would never have believed it!

But it *did* happen. Like a dream come true.

Cormack had been commissioned to write a screenplay around a little-known book by F. Scott Fitzgerald which was set in France's spectacular capital.

For two months he isolated himself from everyone he knew and rented a roomy but fairly basic apartment at the top of an old building which had views of the city to die for.

He mixed solely with the locals, and in eight weeks went from speaking a smattering of restaurant French to being passably fluent—with a very good line in colloquial insults!

For the next two months he infiltrated the expatriate American community in order to get to grips with the characters he was supposed to be writing about. He was fortunate that the American Ambassador just happened to think he was the greatest thing since sliced bread, and introduced

Cormack to just about every influential American living in Paris!

At the end of it all, his research completed, Cormack was mentally and physically exhausted, and sought a few days of winding down before he went back to his home in Malibu to write his screenplay.

Sitting at a table outside a pavement café in the glory of springtime Paris, Cormack sipped at his demi-tasse of coffee and watched the world amble by, relieved to feel some of the tension ebb out of his body—rather like water being slowly let out of the bathtub!

Immune to the polished sophistication of the native Frenchwomen, he was momentarily arrested by the vision of a woman so tall and so fragile that for a second he blinked, as if he had conjured up a creature from another world.

She was dressed in simple black jeans and white T-shirt, with a matching black denim jacket slung casually over her shoulder. A huge-brimmed straw hat covered with masses of violets was crammed down over her head, and the vibrant colour of the flowers contrasted dramatically with the almost translucent paleness of her skin.

She sat down at the table next to his, but did not appear to notice him—and Cormack was excellent at spotting women who merely pretended not to notice him—and he was fascinated by her abstracted air and her fey, understated beauty.

She pulled a book out—in *English*, Cormack noted with pleasure—and opened it up, but he was aware that her eyes gazed sightlessly at the pages. When the waiter came to take her order, she struggled so delightfully to instruct him in French that Cormack was enchanted to play the role of translator—and within ten minutes he managed to charm his way through the barrier of suspicion she had erected enough to share her table with her and, eventually, to get her to agree to dine with him that evening.

When he arrived to collect her at the hotel, she looked absolutely stunning, with her hair caught back in a soft French plait and wearing beautifully understated black jersey. Every Frenchman's eyes narrowed lustfully at the sight of her, while Cormack could not remember feeling quite so elated at being out with a woman.

They ate mussels and rare steak and drank robust red wine in a bistro on one of the tiny uphill streets which stood beneath the mighty shadows of the Notre Dame. He found her relative innocence entrancing and she, in turn, was captivated by his lazy manner, which did nothing to disguise his rather awesome intellect.

They were on their second cup of coffee, with neither of them showing any particular desire to leave, when he asked her, very casually, 'How much longer are you going to be in Paris?'

At that moment Triss cursed her job, and the commitments which went with it. 'I leave tomorrow,' she told him reluctantly, her huge eyes gleaming gold as they reflected the candlelight.

'Pity,' was all he said.

'Yes,' she agreed, and left it at that. Maybe he had someone back in the States? A man like Cormack couldn't possibly be *single*, for heaven's sake!

'Let's go, shall we?' he said suddenly, and Triss felt a fierce rush of regret that the evening had to end.

Outside the restaurant, the moon was a gilded crescent decorating a star-splintered sky, and Cormack turned to her and said, 'It's a warm night. Shall we forget about the taxi and walk back to your hotel?'

'Yes.' She smiled instantly, then wondered if he was expecting to sleep with her. No *way*, she thought ardently as she stole a glance at that dark, craggy profile. However tempting she might find the prospect.

They talked non-stop on the journey back—about politics and art and whether it was time to legislate against motor cars in major cities—this after a speeding vehicle narrowly missed careering into Cormack's shins.

He knew that she was a model—just as she knew that he was a scriptwriter—but in the heady anonymity of the blossom-strewn Parisian streets, their other lives seemed curiously unconnected.

And unimportant.

Some sixth sense warned Cormack to behave with the utmost propriety—indeed, he did not even attempt to kiss her as he left her at her hotel, though he sensed that that was what she wanted him to do more than anything else.

And when he *did* kiss her, at the airport the following afternoon, the world spun on its axis. They both stared at each other in silent amazement afterwards, as if they could not quite believe what had happened, and when he asked her to visit him in Hollywood she shyly said 'OK' without really thinking about it.

When Triss arrived back home in England, the episode seemed more like a dream than reality, and she waited to see what he would do next. If anything.

He sent a book.

Not flowers, but a novel he thought she might find 'interesting'. He was the first man ever to acknowledge her mind rather than her model-girl looks, and Triss was absurdly flattered.

She read the book, was provoked and stimulated by it, and wrote back to tell him so.

He sent another. And another. And then a letter, with an accompanying open-ended air ticket, explaining that he was tied up with a film but that he would love to see her.

Triss did not know which of them was more surprised when she turned up unannounced one day at his Malibu home, and he opened the front door to her wearing ink-splattered white jeans—and nothing else.

There was a long pause.

Well, Triss supposed that *someone* ought to fill the growing silence. 'H-hello,' she said nervously.

He knew much more about her by then. He had asked his agent to come up with anything he hap-

pened to have on a Triss Alexander and had been
unprepared for the shock of realising that the sultry
siren with the flaming mane of hair she had always
kept tame in Paris was the fey, pale beauty who
had captivated his imagination.

'Hi,' he said, very slowly. 'So why didn't you tell
me you were a world-famous supermodel,
Beatrice?'

Triss had done her homework too. 'And why
didn't you tell me that *you* were the *enfant terrible*
of the film world?'

He rubbed at his darkened chin thoughtfully, and
Triss found herself simultaneously wondering
whether he had shaved that morning and whether
or not he intended inviting her in.

'Does it make a difference, then?' he quizzed.

Triss shook her head—today her hair was pleated
into an elegant chignon with not a single strand out
of place. 'Not to me. And you?'

'No.' He stared at her, then suddenly, and without
warning, lifted his hand to the back of her head,
where he located the pin which held the elaborate
hairstyle together and slowly pulled it out, so that
the thick, abundant tresses tumbled down the side
of her face like a Titian waterfall. She heard him
suck in an appreciative breath, saw the way his eyes
darkened in approbation.

Her mouth trembled, colour washing over her
skin as she realised how much she had missed him.
'Aren't you going to invite me in?' she asked, with
a boldness which astonished her.

'Only if you understand that if you set foot over this threshold you're going to end up in my bed. Probably within the hour—that's if I can hold out that long.'

If anyone else had said it she would have run a mile, but when Cormack said it...well, hadn't he just put into words what she had been secretly thinking, secretly hoping for...?

But Triss wanted more than a one-night or one-afternoon stand with Cormack, and instinct told her that tumbling into his bed right now might not be the most sensible thing to do.

So she turned her enormous hazel eyes up at him and smiled, aware and glad for the first time in her life of the sexual power unleashed by that smile. 'Well, in that case,' she murmured smokily, 'you'd better get dressed, hadn't you? And when you've done that you can take me out for lunch. I'll wait in the car.' And she turned on her heel without another word.

Cormack was smitten.

He ached like a schoolboy during lunch at his favourite restaurant, where today the food tasted as uninspiring as school dinners. He wanted her so badly.

He had brought her here to try and impress her, but now he cursed himself for his stupidity, resenting the Hollywood big names who trooped over to their table to say hello, wanting above all else to be away from here, so that he could be alone with her again.

Except that he had probably blown it with his crass approach back at the house.

He couldn't *believe* that a man of his age and with his experience could have come out with a line like that!

Finally they stood up to leave, bathed in golden sunlight, oblivious to the other diners who watched them so closely, completely unaware of the striking sight they made as a couple.

'I'll drop you off,' he said heavily, trying to smile but failing dramatically. 'Where are you staying?'

And Triss turned bemused eyes upon him, wanting him so much that she was past caring whether or not it was the right thing to say, because suddenly it was the *only* thing to say. 'But I thought I was staying with you,' she said. 'Or at least—that was the impression I got earlier. Was I wrong?'

He smiled then, a heavenly smile, which gave Triss a hint of the pleasures to come. 'Just come here,' he murmured, and pulled her into his arms.

Triss came back to the present to find herself studying Cormack with apparent interest, her shorn head cocked to one side.

It must be the hairstyle which made her look even more delicate than usual, Cormack decided, emphasising as it did the small, neat features and making her eyes look so huge that you could imagine drowning in them.

'You were miles away,' he observed.

'So were you,' she said.

'I was,' he answered softly. 'Literally *and* figuratively.'

'Oh?'

'Remembering how we met...'

'In P-Paris?' She stumbled stupidly over the words.

He gave an impatient kind of laugh and his blue eyes seared into her, as if something had made him very angry indeed. 'Unless my memory is defective and we met somewhere else?'

Triss stood up. She hated it when he adopted that terse tone—it was making her feel at even more of a disadvantage than she already did. And just *how* was she going to tell him about Simon, for goodness' sake?

She stared into the moon-like face of the grandfather clock as though she were looking at the gates of hell, but at least her face was hidden from him. And that gave her the courage to try and find out what had motivated him into coming to see her so readily.

'Why did you agree to come here today, Cormack?'

'I thought I'd already told you that, sweetheart,' he returned softly. 'I was intrigued.'

Triss sucked in her breath impatiently. 'Then let me rephrase the question. What did you expect to happen when you got here? Another night of "spectacular sex", as you so sweetly put it?'

'You're surely not complaining because I saw fit to praise your undeniable talents between the sheets?'

She could hear the mocking laughter in his reply. 'Don't twist my words—'

'I'm not twisting anything,' he retorted, his voice laden with an undertone of silky menace. 'But I would be a liar if I denied that I still wanted you, Triss...'

She closed her eyes in despair as she recognised that despite everything which had happened between them she still wanted him too. So badly.

Cormack had risen noiselessly to his feet and had moved behind her, so close that all Triss could hear was the hushed sound of his breathing.

'You're all tense, Beatrice,' he observed quietly, but there was a husky note which deepened his voice into pure allure. 'Aren't you?'

She knew that tone—knew what it meant. Cormack wanted her; she could tell from the barely contained edge of hunger shivering in his voice. But then, he always had been the kind of man who could go from normality to desire within seconds...

'No,' she answered firmly, aware that she should move away from him. But she couldn't. *Couldn't*. 'I'm not tense at all.'

'Oh, yes, you are, sweetheart—you're stretched as tightly as the string of a violin.' Now he sounded cajoling, using the kind of voice she imagined people must use when they were gentling horses.

'N-no.' Then, with a hint of desperation in her voice, she said, 'Stop it, Cormack. Please stop it right now.' But although her words sounded tough enough she still could not bear to turn round, to be confronted by the hot blue dazzle of lust in his eyes. For if she faced *that*—then would she not just give in and fall eagerly into his arms?

Cormack did not answer her immediately, just ran his finger very deliberately down the entire length of her long neck, and the effect of his touch on her skin was electric. 'Just like a swan, that neck,' he mused quietly. 'With its pure, clean lines. A thoroughbred.' He stroked sensually at the soft skin. 'That's what you are, Triss. A thoroughbred.'

She shivered at that first contact and felt the memories flooding back—wonderful, unwanted memories that she had tried to erase from her mind for longer than she cared to remember.

Like the first time they had made love.

She remembered shyly telling him that he was the first man for her, thrilled beyond belief to see the look of dark pleasure on his face. In the back of her mind, however, she had been expecting some kind of pain or discomfort—the stuff they always warned you about in all the books she had ever read on the subject.

But Cormack had been so gentle in his passion, such a slow, sure tutor, that she had experienced nothing but the most perfect kind of fulfillment. She had wept in his arms afterwards, her head cradled on his chest. And he had stroked her dark red hair thoughtfully, but had been remarkably quiet for once.

And she remembered the time when he had given her a key to his Malibu beach home, recalling how she had burst out laughing at the tragi-comic expression on his face and how he had then started laughing too, telling her that he was mourning his lost freedom. And with that shared laughter nothing in the world had seemed to matter outside themselves.

Triss felt rooted to the spot now, in that cramped and overcrowded sitting room, with Cormack gently stroking the back of her neck, aware that every second which passed was weakening what little resolve she had left.

'Come,' he urged softly, and turned her round to face him. 'Come here to me, Triss, sweetheart.'

And Triss felt her breath catch painfully at the back of her throat as she stared at him.

She had seen Cormack in many guises—in jeans and scruffy when he was working flatout on a script, in exquisitely cut chinos and shirts of softest lawn when he was taking her out to lunch, or reluctantly tuxedoed for an obligatory awards night. And yet she could never remember him looking more gorgeous or more desirable than he did right now.

But it was more than the striking vision he made, with his dark, tousled hair and the faintly sinister appeal of the black leather he wore. It was the realisation that Simon was going to grow up to be the spitting image of his father.

So tell him, she thought. *Tell* him! That's why you brought him here today, isn't it?

She stared into his blue eyes, appalled when she read the answering glint there.

'Don't look so horrified,' he murmured. 'There's nothing wrong with wanting me to kiss you...'

'I don't—' she started, but it was too late, because he had pulled her into his arms with an urgency she was not used to. Cormack had always taken great pleasure in his ability to control the pace of their lovemaking. He had always seen the delay of his own sexual gratification as something which gave him immense satisfaction. But this kiss was something else—she had never seen Cormack look so rapt and so absorbed and so *hungry*.

He brought his lips down hard and powerfully against hers, crushing her in his arms so that she could feel his heart beating against her breast—the rapid thundering seeming to symbolise life itself—and Triss found that she was shaking quite violently.

Cormack lifted his head and frowned. 'Why, you're trembling, Triss,' he observed, his own voice sounding slightly unsteady.

'I know. Silly, isn't it?' She rested her head against his shoulder and it felt as though all the troubled times which had passed between them had never occurred. And she was aware that once she told him about Simon she would not have the opportunity to do this again.

'Why?' he questioned softly. 'Why are you trembling?'

Tricky, this one. If she told the truth would she not be revealing her vulnerability where he was concerned? And if she was vulnerable he would be able to hurt her even more than he already had done.

'Triss?' he prompted gently.

'Because it's been so long,' she admitted reluctantly, closing her eyes quickly.

'Since?'

'Since I've ... been intimate with anyone.'

'How long?' he questioned sharply.

'Since—that night.' The night when their son had been conceived.

There was a long, telling silence, and when he spoke his voice sounded unaccustomedly heavy. 'Me too.'

It should have made her burst with joy, but it had the opposite effect—for it made what she had to do even harder.

He bent his mouth to hers once more, and even as she found her lips opening beneath the persistent coaxing of his she wondered when she might gather together enough courage to tell him about Simon.

CHAPTER THREE

TRISS came up for air, though it wasn't easy when all she wanted was for Cormack to carry on kissing her like that. In that mad, passionate way—as though he had just discovered kissing for the very first time. 'Cormack!' she gasped.

'Not now!' he growled, and lowered his head again.

And oh, the sweet power of that kiss threatened to submerge her in its tantalisingly sensual waters. Triss struggled back to reality with difficulty. 'Cormack, please—'

'You don't have to beg me, Triss, sweetheart,' he murmured, with a trace of that hateful irony. 'The pleasure is all mine, I can assure you.'

'But...' Oh, it was hopeless! Hopeless! Triss found her head tipping back, giving Cormack greater access to her neck, which he was now covering with tiny, tiny butterfly kisses so exquisitely delicate that they made her shudder with frustrated longing.

'Triss,' he groaned, and shaped the palms of his hands voluptuously down the sides of her body, as if he were a sculptor creating and forming her out of pliant clay. 'Beautiful, beautiful Triss. God, but you feel good. So good that I want to eat you up.'

Triss fought feelings of intense desire and intense frustration, frantically sucking in air through her mouth as Cormack cupped one of her breasts through the linen dress she wore. She had forgotten just what a master he was at this. If men could take a course on how to drive a woman out of her head with wanting then Cormack Casey would graduate with honours!

Her hips began to move distractedly, as if of their own accord. Tiny, rhythmical little circles, just designed to bring her into contact with the unmistakable evidence of Cormack's growing passion.

This had not been what she had planned. She was supposed to feel *angry* with Cormack, for heaven's sake. He had let her down in every which way.

She had brought him here today solely with the intention of informing him that he was the father of her child. She had planned to tell him not coldly, or judgmentally, just matter-of-factly. As a teacher would explain something to a class.

But nothing more than that—certainly not this. She ran her tongue over her parched lips in despair as she felt her nipple peak beneath the kneading movements of his fingertips.

She tried one last time. 'Cormack, this is wrong...'

He stopped then, lifting his dark head to stare at her accusingly, and she found herself dazzled by the brilliance of his blue gaze. 'No!' He halted her with a negation that was almost savage. 'Whatever else may have happened between us this was never wrong...never could be wrong...You know that, Triss. In your heart you cannot deny it.'

She gave up. It was too much to ask—to deny herself what she wanted more than anything else in the world. And why *not* now? Why not this one, last, glorious time?

Because Triss knew with a certainty which sickened her that Cormack would not make love to her ever again—not once she told him about Simon.

For he was the father of her child. And she knew Cormack well enough to know in her heart that not only would he be livid with her for having concealed that fact, but that he would find it impossible to forgive her for having kept his baby a secret from him for so long.

But hadn't that been her intention? To hurt him as he had hurt her? What some people might have called revenge, but what she had convinced herself was only right and fair.

'Triss, let me make love to you,' he coaxed. 'What we have between us is too good to throw away. Sure, isn't it a crime not to when we feel this way about each other?' And all the while he spoke he was sliding those sensuous fingers over her breasts with such unerring accuracy.

Perhaps another woman with more backbone than Triss might have halted those delicious caresses...might have stopped him from inciting each exquisitely aroused nipple into honeyed life. Would a woman who had not fallen so completely under Cormack's spell have pushed him away?

Well, Triss was certainly not pushing him away. Instead she was kissing him back. Frantically. Almost as frantically as she scrabbled to unzip his leather jacket, to reveal the muscle-packed chest which the grey cashmere sweater could not disguise.

Her hands burrowed right up beneath his sweater and she homed straight in on those tiny, flat nipples, stroking them in the teasing way he had always adored—and the familiar and intimate touch felt like coming home after a long, long journey.

'Sweet Lord in heaven!' He drew in a long, tortured breath. 'Beatrice...Beatrice. My beautiful Beatrice. Don't you know what you're doing to me, sweetheart?'

His words came at her in a haze; he might have been speaking another language for all the sense she made of them.

She could not speak or hear or think. All she could do was clutch onto him for support while he roughly unbuttoned her linen dress so that her aroused breasts were visible, straining madly against the champagne lace of her brassière.

She was aware of a silence, and a stillness, and she opened her eyes in alarm, wondering why on earth he had stopped *now*. And she disturbed an odd kind of watchfulness on his face as he stared at her body.

'Wh-what *is* it?' she managed, from between lips which felt swollen to twice their normal size. 'What's the matter, Cormack?'

The rapt look of absorption had given way to one of narrow-eyed but unmistakable approval. 'Nothing,' he murmured. 'Nothing at all.'

'Then?'

'Your breasts.' He dipped his dark head to flick his tongue tantalisingly against the champagne lace which was stretched taut over one nipple. 'They've changed.'

'Have they?' she questioned lazily as she allowed him to unclip the bra, so that her breasts sprang free into his waiting hands and he immediately began to caress them.

'Mmm. They're lusher, fuller—they look . . .'

Triss froze as the meaning of his words seeped into her addled brain. Any minute now and he would guess the reason for the change—that she had suckled his baby for the past five months.

But Cormack did not seem to be in the mood for any guessing games—in fact there seemed to be only one thing that he was in the mood for, and he shifted uncomfortably before taking her resolutely by the hand.

'Where's the bedroom?' he demanded, in a voice laden with the heated fragility of sexual tension.

Triss wanted him so much that she could not even summon up the simple co-ordination to lift her hand and point to the far door. 'Over th-there,' she whispered falteringly.

Cormack had always been a man to make instant decisions, and there wasn't a trace of doubt on his face as he led her over to the door and pushed it open with all the force of a barnstorming hero from a stage musical.

He didn't wait, pause, look at her, question her, quiz her or try to reason with her. He simply pushed her down onto the bed and then followed as if it was his every right to do so. And he kissed her and kissed her until the need in her grew unbearable.

'Cormack, please—' Was that really *her* voice? Triss wondered. That husky, sensual pleading sound—was *she* making it?

'Please what?'

'You know what!'

'No, I don't,' he growled as his teeth made provocative little mock-bites on her earlobe. 'Not unless you tell me!'

She sensed that if she put into words what she wanted him to do to her, then she might give away how much she feared she still cared for him—despite all her vows and determination to remain immune to the manipulative rogue!

So where did that leave her?

Vulnerable, that was where.

Now he had freed the rest of the buttons of her dress so that it flapped right open, revealing the high-cut champagne lace panties which matched her bra. She brought her knees up instinctively to cover her bare belly, but from the renewed darkening of his eyes she saw that the movement had excited him even more.

'Beatrice,' he groaned. 'You're so lovely. Come here and let me love you.'

And that was her downfall. 'Come here and let me *love* you,' he had said, and Triss allowed herself the foolish luxury of believing him. She went into his arms like an animal seeking refuge from the elements. There she was warm and safe and cosseted.

And very turned on, too. Especially with the flat of his hand roving over her stomach like that.

'Is that good?' he murmured.

If she wasn't going to fight him, she was going to jolly well enjoy him! 'You know it's good,' she answered, on a protesting sigh of enjoyment.

'Do I?' He smiled against her neck.

'Yes.' Her voice sounded slurred as she began to unbuckle the belt of his jeans, and she felt him shudder where her fingers grazed the taut muscle of his abdomen.

'God, that feels like I've just died and gone to heaven,' he sighed.

'Well, don't die just yet,' she teased him.

'Not if you carry on doing that—'

'This?' she whispered provocatively as she began to jerk the protesting zip down.

'Triss, sweetheart,' he moaned. 'Your enthusiasm I love—but if you could find it in your heart to be a little more gentle with me...'

She saw immediately what he meant, and it made her feel strangely shy to be confronted by the very obvious signs of how much he wanted to make love. She found that her fingers had started to falter, and that her cheeks had become stained with a mixture of desire and embarrassment.

She looked down to find that the black leather of his jeans was stretched almost indecently over his arousal, and she suddenly felt an overwhelming need to have him deep inside her.

She felt her body stir into life with the soft, silken rush of desire—instinctively reacting to him in a way she had been half afraid she might have forgotten for ever. But oh, thank heavens, she hadn't.

She felt tears prick the backs of her eyes and found her body trembling uncontrollably, and Cormack must have felt it too, for he halted the slow caress of his lips around the curved line of her jaw to look down at her questioningly.

'What is it, sweetheart? Are those tears I can see?'

She turned her head away. 'No,' she managed, on a broken little gulp.

He turned her head back very firmly. 'Yes,' he contradicted her. 'And what are they for?'

'You'll laugh...'

But he shook his head unhesitatingly. 'Oh, no, I won't,' he told her grimly. 'Believe me when I tell you that I've never felt less like laughing in my life.'

Did that mean he wasn't enjoying himself? Triss found herself wondering nervously, in spite of her emotional state. Wouldn't it be terrible if he decided to stop?

'Tell me, Triss,' he urged softly. 'Please.'

'It sounds so stupid to say it...'

'*I'll* be the judge of that.'

'It's just that this—this *feels* like the first time all over again,' she admitted helplessly, and then

could have kicked herself for leaving herself so raw
and exposed. 'For me, anyway!' she finished, with
a small sniff of defiance.

'For me too,' he told her gently, his gaze very
steady.

She shook her head from side to side. 'You're
just saying that!' she objected. 'You've had so many
women, Cormack, that you probably can't even remember what the first time was like!'

'Yes.' He frowned down at her and his mouth
thinned into a critical line. 'You always *did* have a
rather over-active imagination where my sex life was
concerned.'

'But you're surely not denying—?'

'That I've had other lovers apart from you, Triss?
Oh, no, sweetheart, I'm not denying that. How
could I? But the reality is a lot duller than you might
think. Or do you imagine that I experience the same
kind of mind-blowing reaction to every woman as
I do to you? Well? *Do* you?'

Triss shrugged restlessly, the directness of his gaze
allowing her to acknowledge that in bed, at least,
what they had shared had been unique. 'No,' she
admitted quietly. 'I guess not.'

'And I certainly have not been responsible for
the endless list of conquests which you seem to have
attributed to me!' he finished softly, his blue eyes
crinkling at the corners in that heart-stoppingly cute
way which Triss had always found utterly irresistible. 'Do you understand that, Triss?' he
quizzed softly.

At that precise moment, Triss felt that she had been lured so far into his web of enchantment that all she could do was nod dumbly.

'So...' He kissed the tip of her nose, but she could see the strain of longing which showed on his face. 'Are we going to ruin this by dragging up boring and familiar old arguments?' he queried softly. 'Or are we going to make love?'

It had always been the same. On the one hand Triss was appalled by the outspoken way he came out with things like that...

And on the other?

On the other she thought he was nothing short of wonderful. Still, she realised despairingly. After all this time, the effect he had on her eclipsed just about every other feeling.

Cormack was a man of action. He saw. He asked. He wanted. He took.

And sometimes she took too.

She opened her eyes very wide; their faces were only inches apart. 'We're going to make love,' she told him.

'Well, thank God for that,' he murmured.

Was that triumph she read in the light which flared briefly from the narrowed blue eyes? Suddenly Triss didn't care. She needed Cormack now as never before, to fill this great emptiness inside her.

And afterwards?

Afterwards didn't matter. She would accept the pain if she could just taste the pleasure one last time.

'Cormack—' she said, but she could hear the tremor in her voice and she recognised how tense she still was.

'Shh,' he soothed, and gathered her in his arms— not to begin removing her clothes, as she might have expected, but instead to lay her head against his chest, and to stroke her hair in that rhythmical way of old.

It was both comforting and sensual, and Triss felt all the tension slowly leaving her body. 'Does it feel strange?' she ventured.

'What?' His voice was deep and reflective. 'Having you in my arms again?'

Triss bit her lip as she told herself firmly not to start wishing that things were different—they weren't, and that was a fact of life. 'You stroking my hair—only there's hardly any hair to stroke!'

She could hear the gentle amusement which softened his voice. 'It's interesting,' he mused. 'I can feel the shape of your head—and it's a very beautifully shaped head, I might add.'

'Is it?' she asked, ridiculously pleased.

'Mmm. Nearly as beautiful as your back.' He moved his hands down to illustrate the point, and the strong fingers began to caress and massage her back through the linen of her dress.

Triss wriggled into the warmth of him, aware that her body was beginning to react to him again. Cormack was very astute, she acknowledged—not for the first time. He had instinctively sensed her apprehension. And he was a master at slowing the pace right down when he needed to.

At least, she had no other lover to compare him with, but her instinct told her that no one could better Cormack Casey when it came to making love.

She had no idea how long they lay there, but she could pinpoint exactly the moment when she began to want him to do something more than just idly stroke at her back like that—much as she liked it. She began to move restlessly against him, but he did not take up her invitation.

Boldly she raised her head and began to seek the smooth curve of his jaw with her mouth, momentarily stilling as she felt the first rough graze of his chin.

'You need a shave,' she murmured automatically.

'I had a shave first thing. And don't pretend, Triss. You like to feel my face rasping roughly against you, don't you? You like it best when it scrapes that silken skin hidden at the tops of your long legs. That exquisite contrast between your soft femininity and my—'

'Hard masculinity?' she interrupted, and let her hand brush fleetingly against the rock-like throb of his desire, thrilled to see his eyes close immediately in almost pained rapture.

'Triss!' he gasped.

'Mmm?' she purred.

He had clearly decided that he had exercised enough restraint, for he simply knelt up on the bed, peeled his grey cashmere sweater over his head and flung it carelessly over his shoulder like a seasoned stripper, treating Triss to the first glimpse of his magnificent bare torso.

Now it was her turn to gasp. He looked harder, somehow, and leaner and... It was difficult to describe, but after fourteen Cormack-starved months he seemed more *vital* than she could remember, and Triss forced herself to blot out the question of why she had not fought harder to keep him...

He gave an arrogant smile at her wide-eyed reaction and then turned his attention to the linen dress. 'Take it off,' he instructed softly.

Triss swallowed. Her co-ordination was shot to pieces, and even while her body was crying out for his possession her intellect despised this mindless yearning which Cormack had always been able to produce in her.

She shook her head, and, even though she had cut her hair off fourteen months ago, at that moment she desperately missed the thick red tresses which would have tumbled over her face at this point. She doubted her ability to breathe right now—let alone take her dress and knickers off! 'No!'

'No?' he questioned, curiosity quietening his deep, lilting voice. 'Want me to do it?'

Her hazel eyes flashed resentful green fire at him. 'You know I do—damn you!'

He laughed softly as he began to pull the linen dress down her arms and then dropped it carelessly to the floor.

'That dress cost me a fortune!' she felt dutybound to inform him.

He shrugged. 'You wasted your money, sweetheart. A body like yours should wear as little as

possible. Like now.' His eyes narrowed and
darkened with a fleeting look of perplexity as his
gaze raked hungrily over her lace-clad body. 'Dear
God, Triss,' he breathed, and she had never heard
his voice sound quite so unsteady before. 'Whatever
you've done to yourself, I like it, sweetheart. I like
it a lot.'

What would he say, Triss wondered as she closed
her eyes to conceal her secret from him, if she flip-
pantly announced that having his baby had been
the prescription for giving her the curves she had
always longed for, but which, paradoxically, had
probably put paid to her modelling career for ever?
'D-do you?' she stammered.

'Mmm...'

But Triss could detect the oddest note in his voice,
something she had never heard before, and her
lashes flew open to find that the blue eyes were
searing into her like sharp, piercing arrows, an unmistakable query in their lapis lazuli depths.

'What is it, Triss?' he questioned softly, and the
tone of that question was a close approximation of
the way he used to speak to her in those early days,
when she had been certain that he loved her—before
schedules and jealousy and scheming women had
left their indelible scars on their relationship.

'Tell me,' he prompted softly.

And even while she knew that this was her opportunity to tell him about Simon she also knew
that she was not going to take it.

For Triss was a woman as well as a mother. And
for the last fourteen months she had quashed every

womanly desire in her body with all the ruth-
lessness of a road-builder chopping down trees.

'Triss?'

'I need you,' she whispered, and that was not a
lie, simply an evasion. And thank God it seemed
enough for him to stop probing any further, for he
gave her a hard, assessing smile as he contradicted
her brutally. 'You *want* me, Triss—there is a difference, you know.'

She opened her mouth to protest, but it was too
late, for he was lowering his dark head to capture
her parted lips with his own and she could have
wept with the beauty of that kiss. She was lost in
it, drowning in it, the reality surpassing even her
memories of his kisses—and she had thought that
she had exaggerated *those*.

But no. They said that your memory could play
tricks, and hers must have been about as devious
as it was possible to be, because nothing, *nothing*
could have prepared her for the great, swamping
surge of feeling which that kiss produced.

'C-Cormack,' she gasped, unable to stop herself
as she put her hands up to his shoulders to pull him
right down on top of her. She no longer cared how
hungry or how desperate she might seem to him,
because right now she was being controlled by a
force far stronger than the idea that perhaps a
woman should not behave this way. Well, this
woman *did*!

'Triss!' he groaned as their bodies collided—hers
so soft and pliant, his so hard and unyielding. 'For
God's sake, Triss—slow down!'

'I can't!' It was almost a sob. 'I *can't*!' As she began to pull the smooth, sleek leather down over his buttocks she felt his hardness grow even more potent, and he ground his hips frenziedly against her, as if he could not stop himself.

'Dear God!' she heard him exclaim, and if her hunger was out of control, then his reaction, too, was frighteningly and beautifully unfamiliar. He levered himself up onto his elbows and stared down at her, his breathing already ragged, his face dark and almost savage, his eyes unrecognisable blackened pools of lust. 'You want it this way?' he demanded.

'Yes.' She trembled as he lowered his mouth to kiss the curve of her jaw, and then reality hit her like a sharp blow as she remembered the repercussions of their last encounter. 'Cormack,' she whispered.

'Mmm?'

'I don't want to get—pregnant . . .' Like the night when Simon had been conceived.

But then she had been foolish and hopeful and naïve. Believing that Cormack intended to resume their relationship, and still so in love with him that she had not given contraception a second thought. With far-reaching consequences . . .

He uttered something soft as he pulled a small packet out of the back pocket of his jeans and impatiently ripped it open.

Triss found herself alternating between despair that she was allowing this to happen to her, when all it was going to do was remind her of what she was missing, and agitation in case it didn't happen.

'Want to put it on for me?' he whispered provocatively, but Triss shook her head again.

Apart from the fact that her hands were shaking too much to be of any use, it would be much too poignant to do something which would remind her so much of past intimacies. When every bit of him had been hers to explore as she pleased.

Sadness and frustration combined to make her body writhe impatiently beneath his, and she heard his soft groan as he moved fractionally away from her to slide the condom on.

But still Triss wouldn't let up. She scraped her fingernails with soft, clawing movements over the hard, high curves of his buttocks, and he made a sound midway between a groan of despair and a low laugh of pleasure.

'You know what's going to happen if you keep on doing that, don't you, sweetheart?'

'Yes.'

'This?' And he moved his hand down, slipping his fingers inside her panties to find her so ready for him that it seemed to take a huge effort of will for him to speak another word.

'This?' he asked unsteadily as his fingers began to move against her.

She bucked beneath his touch, her head falling back against the pillow. 'Yes!' she almost sobbed. 'Yes!'

He ripped the panties apart without compunction, at the same time lowering his head to her breast, tearing at the thin, flimsy lace of her brassière with his teeth. And, just when she thought she might die with the pleasure of it, Triss realised that with his other hand he was freeing himself, that he wasn't even going to bother taking his trousers off...

'C-Cormack?'

But it did not sound like Cormack who answered her. 'You wanted it this way, sweetheart,' he said, in a voice grim and distorted with passion, and then he thrust right into her, filling her with his potency as he began to move with the rhythm which was as old as time itself.

She had never known him so out of control before, but that excited her even more.

It all happened so quickly that Triss barely had time to revel in his possession before the sweet waves began to wash over her, and as her body began to convulse she felt Cormack's orgasm too—and how she wished that he wasn't wearing a condom. Right at that moment, some primitive yearning made her long to feel the wetness of his seed as it spilled inside her.

Afterwards she lay naked in his arms, and a deep sense of sadness and despair flowed through her as she acknowledged how perfectly compatible they seemed to be in bed.

In a way, it might be easier if they weren't. If she weren't so fiercely attracted to him—and he to her—then he would not have started stroking her neck in the sitting room. And she would have remained immune to him even if he had.

And they would not now be lying in each other's arms, listening to the sounds of their breathing and their heartbeats gradually slowing down, like two athletes at the end of a race. He raised his head and Triss was taken aback, hardly recognising the shaken and dazed expression she saw on his face.

'Wow,' he said softly.

Triss stifled a groan, just thankful that she had not built herself up to expect tender words from him. Because, while 'Wow' could reasonably be taken as testimony that Cormack had enjoyed himself, it wasn't a word which was even remotely caring.

And she still had to tell him about Simon.

Fatigue washed through her as she went over the words she had rehearsed over and over in her mind for weeks now, and it was something of a relief when the emotional strain finally took its toll of her body and she allowed her eyelids to drift down.

CHAPTER FOUR

TRISS must have fallen asleep, for when she next opened her eyes it was to find that Cormack was no longer on the bed beside her. Instead he had put on his grey sweater back on, belted up his leather trousers and was sitting in a chair drinking a mug of coffee, a forbiddingly sombre expression on his face.

She quickly shut her eyes again, as if by feigning sleep she could postpone the moment of truth. At least he must have covered her up with this blanket, she thought thankfully, becoming slowly aware of the rips in her brassière and the torn panties which now lay in useless folds halfway down one thigh.

Instinctively she felt her body cringing as vivid impressions of how she had behaved came back with piercing clarity.

'Ashamed, Triss?' came the mocking remark, tinged with a coldness which she had never heard in Cormack's voice before.

She sat up, pulling the blanket with her so that it concealed her breasts, and his mouth twisted scornfully as he acknowledged the self-protective gesture.

'A little late in the day for shielding your assets, surely?' he queried with disdain, and Triss felt her heart sinking with horror as she realised that never—not even when their relationship had reached rock-bottom—had Cormack spoken to her with quite so much contempt hardening his normally soft, lilting Irish accent.

But she could not afford to squander even more emotional energy by allowing herself to be intimidated by his scathing remarks. 'I'm cold,' she told him, noticing that he had picked her linen dress up from the floor and folded it on the chair beside the bed.

A muscle worked in his tanned cheek. 'Try putting some clothes on, then,' he said moodily.

Feigning a bravado she did not feel, Triss swung her legs over the side of the bed. Her panties fluttered redundantly to the floor, and she noticed that he quickly turned away to face the window.

'I'll wait next door,' he told her shortly, and when Triss saw the unmistakable distaste which had thinned his sensual lips a slow anger began to burn away inside her.

'A little late to play the gentleman now, surely?' she mocked.

He turned around to subject her to a slow, insolent scrutiny. 'What's that, Triss?' he queried softly. 'Cue for me to come over there and do it to you some more?'

She recoiled from the wounding words. 'Why are you insulting me like this?'

'Perhaps I'm repaying the compliment, sweetheart! A man doesn't find it particularly flattering to be used as a stud—especially by a woman who once professed to love him. Is that what you brought me here for, Triss—to service you? Surely there must be someone who lives a little closer than Malibu who would be able to oblige?'

She forgot that she was virtually naked, forgot everything except the desire to hurt him, hurling herself across the room and launching herself at him, all flailing arms and flexed fingernails.

But Cormack was faster, his face a mixture of scorn and reluctant desire as he contained her by imprisoning her in the steely circle of his arms. 'Is this another previously undiscovered side to Triss Alexander? The spitting wildcat who needs subduing? And let me guess how she best wants me to subdue her, hmm? Like this?'

His lips were hot and hungry and hers were no different, and Triss found to her despair that just one touch was enough to awaken in her a primitive arousal more powerful than anything she could previously remember.

His hands were sliding all over her almost naked body, quickly disposing of the ruined bra, sinuously exploring every secret curve with an expert thoroughness which he had never displayed before. Not ever.

It was almost as if he had held back with her when they had lived together, as though her inexperience had made him especially gentle with her.

Well, he was certainly not being gentle with her now. And, what was more, she didn't want him to be. She wanted his hands to explore her like this, and she longed for him to fill and possess her again.

She was about to sink to the floor and drag him with her when he stopped kissing and touching her as suddenly as if he had just discovered that she was contaminated, and Triss stared up at him with eyes which were dazed and confused.

'Cormack?'

'No, Triss! *No!* This is not going to happen. Not again.' His voice was pitiless as he pushed her away from him. 'I will not be used as a convenient pawn to satisfy your sexual frustration!'

'But I—'

'Get dressed!' he ordered, and something in his eyes made her want to cringe away from him, like a dog who had been beaten. 'I'll wait next door!' And he stormed from the bedroom, nearly bringing the door off its hinges.

It took Triss several minutes before she could even think about managing to get dressed, and she forced herself to breathe deeply as she had been taught in her yoga classes. Even so, it still seemed to take ages before she had calmed down enough to get her thoughts together.

She hadn't known how long they would be at the cottage, but she had guessed at a good few hours at least, during which time she had planned to tell Cormack quietly about Simon. And then she had assumed that he would want to accompany her back to St Fiacre's for the first glimpse of his son.

But nothing ever turned out as you expected, and she certainly had not anticipated that brief and frantic bout of sex on the bed—for it definitely could not be described as making love.

Oh, it had been ultimately satisfying—sex with Cormack always was—but it had left her feeling empty and ashamed. And it made her feel rather ill to know that she had behaved with about as much pride as one of the countless women who used to hand him their telephone numbers in restaurants.

At least she had had the foresight to bring a change of clothes with her—although as she pulled on a pair of black denims and a cream cable-knit sweater she wondered whether that had been a subconscious preparation for what had just taken place.

She ran her fingers back through her short redbrown hair and walked into the sitting room, to find that Cormack had put his leather jacket back on and was in the process of bending down to pick up his helmet.

'You're not going?' she cried in alarm.

He stood up and looked at her, his face as expressionless as she could ever remember seeing it. 'Yes, I'm going.'

Triss panicked, aware that all her carefully laid plans were crumbling like dust around her. 'But why—why rush off?' she queried, hating the sound of her garbled question.

He raised his eyebrows in a look of incredulity. 'I thought I made my feelings clear a moment ago.'

Offensively clear—but that was not the point. Triss tried to swallow down the panicky feeling which was making her head swim. 'You don't understand!'

He shook his head. 'Oh, I think I do, Triss. And I'm not exactly proud of what just happened.'

Triss frowned, dismayed and baffled by his reaction. And angry too. 'But you enjoyed it, didn't you, Cormack?' she accused him.

His mouth twisted. '*Enjoyed* it?' he echoed. 'I could think of a lot more appropriate words to describe how that rather sordid little coupling made me feel, but I suspect that you might be insulted if I used any of them.'

She tried one last time, biting back the urge to agree with him—and to get as far away from him as possible. 'Cormack, you don't understand—'

'Yes!' he cut in mercilessly. 'I do. That's just the trouble—I understand only too well! We're no good for each other, you and I, Triss! We can't live together—we just destroy each other. The sex between us is mind-blowing—it always was—but at least before there was communication and affection. Even occasional laughter, which inevitably comes when you live together—at least at the beginning,' he finished heavily.

'Cormack, just let me explain—'

He shook his head. 'Hear me out first, Triss. And perhaps that might spare both of us the indignity of something like this happening again. This must be the last time we see each other—*do you understand that? Do* you, Triss?'

He looked at her, his features tightly contained, as if he was determined not to betray one flicker of emotion. 'Since our relationship is finished and all that is left is physical attraction—it diminishes whatever we once had between us—or it will *if* we give in to it. So we won't. And I think that the only way to guarantee that happening is for us not to see one another again.'

She watched as he ran one long forefinger caressingly over the shiny red and silver surface of his helmet in an unconsciously sensual gesture, and then he gazed at her directly, his blue eyes searingly candid.

'I cared for you more than any woman I've ever known, Triss—perhaps more than I ever will in the future. It just didn't work out. That's all. That's life.' He attempted a conciliatory smile, but Triss felt that he might as well have been firing poisoned darts at her.

'At least we didn't make it as far as the altar,' he continued. 'And at least we didn't have children together. We might have messed each other's lives up, Triss, but at least we didn't inflict misery on any defenceless offspring.'

She could not let him say any more. His words had already ripped through what little self-possession she had left and had left her in no doubt whatsoever that their relationship was well and truly over.

Any more of that caustic, wounding tongue of his and Triss really doubted that she would have the strength to go through with what she had brought him here to say. Because already he was turning towards the door, that bitter, angry look still on his face.

'You have a son, Cormack,' she said into the brittle silence.

He stilled.

Triss thought that he might not have heard her. 'You have a son,' she repeated desperately, longing for some—*any*— kind of reaction, then immediately wished that she hadn't, for the outraged look of disbelief on his face was like a sabre being plunged deep into her heart.

Countless seconds ticked by, and when he spoke it was as though he was using unfamiliar words, for his voice was totally unrecognisable. 'Tell me that what I just heard is not true, Triss.'

She swallowed down the acrid taste of despair. 'You have a son,' she said again quietly.

He came across the room like a panther stalking its terrified prey, until he stood just in front of her, his eyes blazing angry blue fire which scorched into her soul. 'You're lying—'

'I wish I was,' she said, and then, when she realised the implications of *that*, '*No!* I didn't mean *that*!' she exclaimed in horror. 'I just meant—'

'Shut up!' He looked angry enough to strike her, but Triss knew that she was safe from violence, for no matter how forceful his rage Cormack was a man who despised physical supremacy when it was abused. One of his finest screenplays had exposed a wife-beater as the lowest form of cringing coward. It had earned him his first Oscar nomination.

'How old is he?' he shot out, and his words had all the cold, penetrating accuracy of a bullet.

'He—he's five months.' She did not need to look at Cormack's fierce expression of concentration to know that he was frantically trying to work out when Simon might have been conceived.

'Oh, he's yours all right, Cormack,' she informed him steadily, trying her utmost to withstand the blast of raw rage which was emanating from his smouldering eyes. 'You have only to look at him to know which stable he came out of.'

'Only you've never given me the opportunity to do that, have you, Triss?' he snarled. 'To look at him?'

'I had my reasons!' she defended herself, aware of how stilted she sounded.

'Oh, *really*?' he bit out in disgust, and Triss almost recoiled from the look of stark hostility he directed at her.

When she had felt lonely and lost, and been missing Cormack like mad, her idea of keeping his child a secret from him had seemed like the ultimate act of justifiable revenge for the ruthless way he had treated her. But now Triss wondered if she had been insane at the time. Had her wildly fluctuating hormones been all over the place, making her temporarily mad enough to try and conceal Cormack's baby from him?

Because if she had stopped to think through all the repercussions properly would she not have anticipated his terrible, terrible rage at finding out in such a way? And what would his next action be? Dear Lord, thought Triss frantically, what on earth had she started here?

'Where is he now?' he snapped.

'At home.'

'And where's home?'

'In Surrey. We've only just moved. We live in a beautiful house in—'

He interrupted her with a harsh demand. 'Who's looking after him now?'

Triss swallowed. All of a sudden she did not feel confident enough to admit to Cormack that she had left their son with a woman she had scarcely known for any time at all.

Lola Hennessy was her next-door neighbour— an air stewardess with a sunny disposition and the sweetest smile that Triss had ever seen. Triss had watched the way that Lola played with Simon, and had known with a woman's unerring instinct that Simon could not be in better hands.

'Lola is looking after him,' said Triss quickly. 'And she's a friend of mine.'

'But not an old friend, obviously, since *I've* never heard of her.' Blue eyes bored into her so accusingly that Triss flinched. 'Can she be trusted?'

'Of *course* she can be trusted!' Triss exploded. 'Do you really think I'd leave my baby—'

'*Our* baby,' he corrected her immediately, his words icy with anger.

'—with someone who can't be trusted?' she finished.

His eyes were spitting angry blue sparks. 'How the hell should I know?' he demanded. 'You didn't even bother to inform me that I *had* a child, which is pretty abnormal behaviour in anyone's book.

Why stop there? Why not engage a group of tame gorillas to look after him?'

She tried to tell herself that it was natural for him to lash out in view of what she had just told him. What she had not expected was for his criticism to hurt quite *this* much. 'Cormack,' she said quietly, 'calm down.'

But he shook his head. 'So tell me,' he went on, his Irish accent deepening, 'how many people are privy to this great secret of yours? Your mother? Your brother? Am I the last to know?'

'Cormack, at least let me try to explain—'

'Keep your explanations!' he snapped. 'Every damned one of them! Because every word you speak sickens me to my stomach. Just get your coat and your things together. We're going.'

'G-going where?' she asked him in confusion.

'To see him, of course!' he retaliated, and he clenched his teeth together in a look which was almost feral. 'I want to see my son!'

Despair warred with futile hope in Triss's heart when she heard the fiercely possessive note in his voice as he spoke about his son. *Already!*

Blue fire burned from his eyes. 'What have you called him?'

'Simon.'

There was a pause while he digested this. 'Simon what?'

Triss swallowed. 'Simon Cormack Patrick,' she got out through lips which felt as though they had been glued together.

Cormack Patrick senior expelled a breath which sounded more like a hiss. 'You bitch,' he said softly. 'You scheming, devious little bitch! What right did you have to give *my* child *my* name—'

'He's my child too!'

'—and yet keep his very existence from me?' He shook his head in dazed disbelief. *'Why?'*

Triss had to bite her lip to stop it from trembling—with indignation as well as shock at the depth of his anger towards her. What right did *he* have to accuse *her* of being scheming and devious when she was fully aware of *his* underhand behaviour and his deceit?

She opened her mouth to sling his insults back at him, but something stopped her. Now was not the time or the place to trade slurs. Let him feel outraged and hurt and isolated instead—for had he not been responsible for imposing that very state on her?

She automatically raked her fingers back through her shorn hair, and she saw Cormack's eyes briefly narrow in a look which was alarmingly close to pain. It was a gesture which harked back to the days when she had needed to push the thick dark red waves away from her face.

Had it reminded him of other, happier times? Triss wondered. Or the exact opposite? 'I don't think that now is either the time or the place to discuss my reasons—'

'For denying me my child?' he flared, his face about as dark as the leather which clung to him.

Triss swallowed down her fear and doubt. Cormack was wounded, yes, as she had intended to wound him, but why did her victory suddenly seem so hollow and empty? She had expected his anger—but she had anticipated nothing on this scale. Nor the genuine hurt and bewilderment which she suspected lay behind his angry words.

She tried to harden her heart against him, but with very little success. 'None of this is getting us anywhere,' she said, in an odd, trembling sort of voice.

'Too damn right it isn't!' he snapped dismissively, and as he looked at her the grim expression on his face filled Triss with a sinking feeling of dread.

For there was nothing but an icy coldness there—a look as unlike Cormack as she had ever seen. It was, she realised, the death of all his feeling for her—other than scorn and dislike.

And Triss knew that she had paid the highest price possible for exacting her revenge on Cormack. Because if ever she had harboured any secret hopes of getting him back she could see from his face that any such hopes were futile . . .

The first part of the journey back to St Fiacre's was conducted in a terse, bitter silence. They took Triss's car but Cormack drove—her hands were shaking too much for her even to be able to consider driving.

'But what about your motorbike?' she had asked him back at the cottage. 'We can't just leave it here.'

His mouth had curved into a disdainful smile. 'I have no intention of just leaving it here. I'll arrange to have it collected and delivered to your house.'

'M-my house?' she stammered. 'But why *my* house?'

He threw her a disbelieving look. 'Because that's where I'm going to be staying for the foreseeable future,' he ground out, and Triss stared at him with real alarm.

Because reaction to their earlier passion was now beginning to set in. And Triss knew that the aching she felt deep inside her was much more than just a physical readjustment to making love after such a long time and having had a baby in the interim.

For, no matter how loveless the union which had taken place on the bed before, Cormack was still the father of her child—still the man she had loved more than she could ever have imagined loving anyone. And she was not immune to him—indeed, she suspected that she never *would* be immune to him.

So how the hell could he suggest staying in her house? And how on earth could she contemplate letting him do so?

'You can't do that!' she protested.

'No?' He raised a dark, arrogant eyebrow. 'Just watch me, Triss.'

'It's *my* house—'

'Listen, sweetheart,' he cut in brutally. 'You can stand there and spout a list of objections as long as your arm, but believe me when I tell you that they will not make an iota of difference to my plans—'

'What plans?' she asked immediately, wondering why all this seemed to be going so horribly wrong.

He shook his dark head. 'I don't intend to waste any more time in discussion now. Just lock up, then get in the car and we'll talk there.' He took her small overnight bag from her and began to trudge up the hard, wet sand towards where Triss had parked her navy BMW.

Triss felt too emotionally overwhelmed to do anything other than automatically carry out his instructions, so she locked up the cottage and made her way towards the car, where Cormack was already settled in the driving seat, his dark profile stony and unforgiving.

She waited until he had negotiated the car up the steep, narrow lanes and was at last heading out on the motorway towards London before she brought the subject up once more.

'What plans,' she asked, 'were you referring to earlier?'

There was a pause. 'Plans to get to know my son, of course.'

'Cormack, I really think—'

'And the only way to do that is to live with him,' he continued remorselessly.

His words were like lethal little darts being fired into her skin—there was such unconcealed venom behind them. 'Live with him?' she questioned faintly, not quite believing what she'd heard, but the implacable expression in his blue eyes left her in no doubt.

'Yes, live with him!' he echoed passionately. 'Because you've denied me five months of his life, damn you, Triss Alexander, and I don't intend to let you deny me any more!'

Triss closed her eyes and saw a vivid image of what living with a Cormack who despised her might be like, and she felt physically sick at the thought of it. 'You can't just *barge* into someone's house uninvited—'

'But you *did* invite me, didn't you?' he told her in that silky Irish way of his as he smoothly overtook a car which was hogging the middle lane. 'If not to your house, then certainly back into your life. And there must have been a reason behind that invitation, mustn't there, sweetheart?'

His eyes glittered with undisguised hostility. 'So what was it? Getting tired of the burden of motherhood? Wanting to spread your wings? Some man on the horizon who can't tolerate the sound of a crying baby when he's trying to make love to you?'

'If you weren't driving I would hit you for saying something as disgusting as that!' she fired back at him, her heart thudding painfully in her chest.

He shrugged, seemingly unperturbed by her threat. 'Disgusting, Triss?' he mocked. 'Or realistic?'

'Do you really *think*,' she flared, so angry that she could barely catch her breath, 'that I would have gone to bed with *you* this afternoon if I had some other man hovering in the background?'

He edged smoothly into top gear and the powerful car seemed to swallow up the road in front of them. 'How would I know *what* you would do any more?' he challenged fiercely. 'You're like a stranger to me now, Triss.'

'A *stranger*?' she whispered, slowly becoming aware that her actions seemed to have opened up a real can of worms. She had seen no further than her desire to hurt Cormack as he had hurt her; she had given no thought to how she still felt about the father of her baby. And no thought, either, to how vulnerable his blistering criticism would make her feel. 'Cormack—I shared your life and your house for almost a year...'

His mouth hardened forbiddingly at the corners. 'If you think that I am about to be swayed by your sentimental reminiscences, then think again, sweetheart!' he snapped, speaking with a bitter kind of cynicism which Triss had never heard him use before.

'So how can you say that I'm like a stranger to you?' she asked him in genuine confusion.

'Because the woman I thought I was in love with would never have behaved in such a despicable way!' he stormed. 'You suddenly confront me with the news that I am a father—'

'And have you never stopped to ask yourself just *why* I might have behaved in such a "despicable" way?' Triss snapped back as she remembered how she had felt when she'd discovered that he had betrayed her.

He shook his dark head impatiently. 'I'm afraid that your motivations concern me less than practical considerations at the moment, Triss. Like whereabouts in Surrey are we going?'

She wondered whether he would have heard of it. 'To St Fiacre's Hill estate,' she told him slowly.

He had. He exhaled a long, low breath. 'Not "The Beverly Hills of England"?' he quoted, in a mocking sing-song voice.

'That's what the tabloids say,' answered Triss, with a defensive little shrug.

'And the reason why, presumably, you wanted to live there?'

The numbing effect of the intimacies they had shared was wearing off, and now came the return of Triss's sense of purpose. 'Don't make any presumptions on my behalf, thank you very much!' she told him frostily. 'I happened to buy the house because it is set in almost nine hundred acres of beautiful green land.'

'Rather than because it happens to be populated by rich men with an eye for a beautiful woman on her own?' he mocked.

'That doesn't even deserve the courtesy of a response!' Triss glared at him. 'St Fiacre's is secure and well tended and very, very private. And the gates keep unwelcome visitors out—'

'Like me?' he queried sardonically.

Triss went quiet.

'That must have influenced your choice of where to live?' he suggested softly. 'I imagine that if your instantly recognisable face—'

'But I'm *not* instantly recognisable any more!' she protested. 'I've had my hair cut off—remember?'

'Maybe not instantly,' he conceded. 'But certainly recognisable. Not many women have eyes and bone-structure and height and posture like yours, Triss. If you had chosen to live anywhere else I shouldn't think it would have been too long before someone was tempted by the lure of money from one of the newspapers to tell the story of the super-model turned single mother.' His blue eyes glittered. 'With a lot of speculation as to who the absentee father might be.'

Triss gave a silent groan as she remembered blurting out Cormack's identity to Lola. But she trusted Lola.

'But I *presume*,' he continued remorselessly, 'that everyone who lives on St Fiacre's is so financially secure and so paranoid about their *own* safety that they've barely given you a second look. And even if they did they certainly wouldn't need to flog your story for cash.'

Triss wondered whether this whole idea of telling Cormack about his son had been nothing more than a hare-brained scheme. But it was too late to back out now. 'You need to take the furthest exit on this roundabout,' she told him in an odd, brittle kind of voice that did not sound like her voice at all. 'We're almost there.'

CHAPTER FIVE

As CORMACK drove through the wrought-iron gates of St Fiacre's, with their distinctive navy- and gold-painted crest, Triss thought that she had never seen the estate look more beautiful or more welcoming.

It was a brilliantly sunny early March afternoon, and clumps of daffodils swayed in bright yellow patches beneath the hundreds of trees which lined the roads.

Few of the houses were visible—protected by lush shrubbery and drives which seemed to go on for ever—but occasionally they caught sight of a drift of smoke from a chimney, or heard the muffled barking of a dog.

The happiness which settled upon her whenever she entered the serene green beauty of St Fiacre's stole over her, and Triss found herself brightening in spite of everything that had happened. She thought of Simon and hugged her shawl round her shoulders excitedly, her eyes shining brightly at the prospect of seeing her baby again.

Cormack shot her a swift glance. 'You've missed him.'

It was less a question than an astute statement, and Triss nodded. 'Yes,' she answered quietly. 'I've missed him like crazy, if you must know.'

He opened his mouth to say something else, then halted as they heard the sound of an approaching engine, which even Triss—who was not remotely interested in cars—could tell powered one hell of a machine.

She almost smiled when she saw Cormack's eyes narrow with male competitiveness. A long, low Aston Martin in dark and gleaming green slowed down as it passed them, before roaring off towards the main gates.

'That's just like *your* car!' Triss pointed out in surprise.

Cormack's expression tightened. 'Now what the hell is *he* doing here?'

Triss craned her neck to make out who was driving and saw a handsome but disturbingly cruel face, set into grim and determined lines. And for some reason a shiver began to whisper cool fingers all the way down her spine. 'Who?'

'Dashwood,' answered Cormack succinctly, a frown pleating his forehead above the dark sweep of his brows.

'Not *Dominic* Dashwood?' queried Triss, turning back to get a better look at him over her shoulder.

'So you do know him?'

'I know *of* him,' Triss corrected him icily, not liking that judgmental look on Cormack's face one little bit. 'Doesn't everyone?'

'Surely not *another* member of the Dashwood fan club?' came the sardonic jibe.

Triss fixed him with a long-suffering look. 'When a man is that rich and that good-looking, most people get to hear of him.'

'But Dashwood's proximity naturally had *nothing* to do with your buying a house here?'

'Oh, for goodness' sake!' Triss exploded. 'Why should it?'

'Husband-hunting, perhaps?' Cormack suggested insultingly.

Taking a deep breath, Triss resolved to keep her cool. 'I'm not in the market for a husband,' she told him with icy emphasis.

'No?'

'No.'

'I don't know that I believe you, Triss,' he accused softly.

She forced her voice to sound very faintly bored. 'I'm afraid that your beliefs are *your* problem, Cormack. Nothing to do with me. You have to turn left here, by the way.'

He complied without a word, although Triss heard him draw in an appreciative breath when he caught his first glimpse of her thirties-style house, with its stained-glass windows and its oak door, and its red-brick walls covered with newly budding wisteria.

'Is Simon here?' he demanded as the car drew to a halt by the front door.

'He's next door at Lola's. I'll let you in, shall I, and then go and fetch him?'

'Oh, no,' said Cormack grimly. 'I'm fascinated to meet this "friend" of yours, whom you see fit to entrust with the care of our son. You must think very highly of her, if you grant her a privilege you've denied me.'

'I don't want you coming in there with me if you're intending to make trouble,' Triss warned.

'I just want to see him, Triss.' His searingly blue eyes blazed a question at her. 'Surely even *you* can understand that?'

His appeal came straight from the heart, and Triss felt utterly wretched at that moment. She nodded dumbly.

'Then let's go,' he ordered quietly.

They walked silently, side by side, but that was their only concession to togetherness. The tension and the animosity sizzled between them like sparks crackling from a bonfire. They passed through Triss's informal gardens and into the rather more elaborate plantings of Lola Hennessy's house next door.

Cormack raised his eyebrows as he took in the imposing white building which made Triss's house seem almost tiny in comparison. 'This is some place,' he commented drily. 'Your friend Lola is clearly a successful woman. What does she do?'

Lola was an air hostess who had inherited the house from a wealthy man almost forty years her senior. But if Triss told Cormack *that* he would start leaping to all sorts of unsavoury conclusions! And, quite honestly, Triss was finding the situation difficult and fraught enough, without fanning the flames of his contempt even further.

Anyway, Lola *was* successful though not in the way that Cormack meant. She had a job she adored, a busy social life and the fulfilment of working with one of the country's most popular charities. She also had an outrageously attractive Welshman named Geraint Howell-Williams hovering in the background, though Triss was aware that he had been giving Lola considerable problems.

They reached the front door, which was flung open before either of them had a chance to knock. In the hall stood a young woman in her twenties wearing leggings and a loose denim shirt. Her gloriously curly dark brown hair was tied up with a red chiffon scarf, although wayward curls were escaping everywhere, and her bright blue eyes sparkled like gems in the sunshine.

'Triss, *hi*!' she exclaimed, with a huge smile. 'I saw you coming down the path! We just weren't expecting you back so soon!' She looked from one to the other, the smile dying as she must have registered the decidedly frosty atmosphere between the two of them.

'We—we wanted to get back,' stuttered Triss awkwardly. 'Is everything OK?'

'Everything is fine—'

'How's Simon?' asked Triss quickly.

'Simon's just *wonderful*,' Lola reassured her firmly. 'I can hardly bear to give him back to you. Come and see.'

Triss forced herself to try and act normally, though she found herself stupidly wondering whether it was obvious that she and Cormack had spent the afternoon in bed together. She could feel the unusually high colour in her cheeks which would not seem to fade. 'This is Cormack Casey,' she said, rather hesitantly.

Lola held her hand out immediately. 'Hello, Cormack.' She dimpled, as if it were every day that she met friends' estranged lovers who happened to be world-famous scriptwriters! 'I saw your last film three times! I loved it—especially the bit where she discovered that the letter had never been sent.'

Triss watched the stiff set of Cormack's shoulders relax. She knew that he had been suspicious, and prepared to dislike Lola—and perhaps that was understandable in the circumstances—but no one could help but warm to someone who was so friendly and unaffected. And who was clearly a fan!

'Did you, now?' he queried, though his smile looked forced. 'I'm Simon's father,' he told her bluntly.

Triss looked anxiously at Lola, who was already aware of this fact, but to her credit she merely nodded, as if people confided their paternity every day of the week, and said, 'I see.'

'How is he?' asked Triss again. 'How has he been?'

'Wonderful! A textbook baby! But don't just take *my* word for it—come and see for yourself! He's been out for a walk,' Lola informed them as they followed her across the magnificent entrance hall towards a set of carved-oak double doors. 'Then he had a bottle. And my mother watched over him while he had his snooze.' At Triss's raised eyebrows she said quickly, 'She's upstairs at the moment, resting—I'll tell you about it later. We were just thinking of giving Simon some tea. He's in here...'

She pushed the door open and Triss felt all Cormack's tension return as he saw his baby being cradled in the arms of a tall man who was a total stranger to him.

At the sound of the door being opened the man turned to face them, and Simon immediately let out a huge gurgle of joy when he saw Triss.

'Oh, Geraint!' laughed Lola, her voice sounding slightly dreamy. 'He's been sick all over your shoulder!'

Stormy grey eyes glanced dismissively at some regurgitated milk which had splodged over the shoulder of a black cashmere sweater, then the man shrugged. 'It'll wash,' he drawled, in a distinctively Welsh accent.

Without another word he walked across the room, carrying a wriggling Simon who was holding his arms out and trying to launch himself out of Geraint's grip. 'Hi, Triss,' he said gently. 'Have your boy back.' And he handed Simon over to Triss.

The baby locked his chubby arms around Triss's neck and immediately began to squirm happily against her.

'Hello, darling,' Triss whispered softly, closing her eyes briefly as she rubbed her chin against the delicate silk of his black hair, unaware that Cormack was standing across the room from her, watching her and watching Simon, his blue eyes narrowed and assessing.

An awkward silence fell, and Triss was wondering just what to do next when Geraint came to her aid by moving across the room to stand rather proprietorially beside her.

He held his hand out towards Cormack. 'Geraint Howell-Williams,' he said.

The two men eyed each other warily, like two prime predators sizing each other up, then shook hands—though Cormack continued to subject Geraint to a steady, curious stare. 'Cormack Casey.'

'I know who you are.'

'Then you have the advantage over me,' said Cormack, his normally lilting Irish accent sounding harsh and abrasive. 'Because I don't know *you* from Adam!'

'I'm going to marry Lola,' said Geraint, by way of an explanation, looking directly into Cormack's eyes.

'I don't remember agreeing to announce it!' protested Lola, though her smile was so wide it threatened to split her face in two.

'Don't you?' queried Geraint in a teasing drawl. 'Well, I do—but you clearly had other things on your mind, darling!'

'*Geraint!*' Lola blushed a deep scarlet, but the look which passed between the two of them was electric with warmth and love and an uninhibited sexual tension.

And we used to be like that, thought Triss, an unbearable sadness sweeping over her as she remembered a time when she and Cormack had both been incandescent with love. When just a shared look across a crowded room had been enough to make every other person fade into insignificance.

She had to get out of here before she did something unforgivable—like breaking down in tears in front of everyone. She hugged Simon even closer to her chest, and he gave a mildly protesting wriggle.

'We'd better be going,' she said quickly. 'Thank you so much...'

But Lola was already gently pushing her in the direction of the door. 'You don't have to thank us,' she said softly. 'It was our pleasure. Just go,' she whispered, so that only Lola could hear. 'And sort some things out between you.'

Cormack did not say a word as the three of them walked back towards Triss's house.

Triss sneaked a look at him. She had never seen him look quite so dazed. He was staring at the baby clasped closely against her chest with the same kind of rapt scrutiny he would have given a statue which had just been brought to life in front of him.

He looked, she thought, like a man taking part in a dream sequence—as though none of what was happening made very much sense to him.

Come to think of it, events had a pretty bizarre quality for her too.

Once inside the house, she went straight into the kitchen. 'Here,' she said, and handed the baby to him. 'You hold him for a bit. Don't worry, he's very good; he often goes happily to—' She stopped abruptly, her eyes widening with horror as she realised what she had been about to say.

'Strangers?' he supplied, with acid emphasis.

'I'm sorry, I didn't mean—'

'Please don't apologise,' said Cormack, in a crisp kind of authoritative voice he had never used with her before. 'It's nothing more than the truth.' And then he bent his dark head to concentrate all his attention on the warm, curious bundle in his arms.

He held Simon gingerly at first, as if he had been given an incredibly precious burden to carry. Then, after a little while, he sat down on one of the high stools at the breakfast bar, still clutching the child to him, and Simon just stared up at his father with interested, identical deep blue eyes.

Triss turned away and busied herself in an effort to stem the tears she found inexplicably pricking at her eyes. Of *course* they look the same, she told herself fiercely, swallowing down the infuriating salt taste at the back of her throat. But just because the two of them look as though they should be auditioning for a happy-families soap-powder commercial it does not mean that everything is now hunky-dory.

She boiled the kettle and made a pot of tea, then took some mashed potato and broccoli from the fridge and began to warm it through.

When the dish was prepared she looked round to find that Simon had lifted a podgy hand and was tugging at a strand of thick black hair which had flopped onto Cormack's forehead. But it was the expression on Cormack's face which turned her heart to stone.

For he had removed his tender gaze from Simon to stare across the kitchen at her, and the withering look of contempt on his face was like a knife-wound to the heart.

'What right did you have,' he asked slowly, each word seeming to be torn from somewhere deep inside him, 'to deny me this?'

Her mouth wobbled, but she would not cry—she would *not*. 'I don't want a scene now,' she told him, with a quiet dignity that cost her an effort. 'Not now and not here. Not in front of Simon. It will only confuse him.'

His answering words were soft; only their meaning was as bitter and as abrasive as a physical blow. 'And you don't think you've confused him enough already?' he accused her. 'Leaving him with someone you barely know? You think it's acceptable for Geraint Howell-Williams to hold him and to know him, do you, Triss? Some guy who has the most tenuous connection with his life? While I'm just left like the spectre at the feast— grabbing what small crumbs of him you see fit to throw my way?'

She felt unspeakably weary, as if her head had suddenly become too much for her slender neck to be able to hold. 'I said not now, Cormack,' she repeated, in a low voice which trembled unsteadily with strain as she watched Simon's head turn from one to the other of them in bewilderment. Their voices had not been raised, but the bitterness behind

their words was unmistakable. 'Rowing in front of
Simon is the last thing either of us wants or needs
right now.'

He made a small sound of disgust. 'Don't you
dare have the temerity to talk about *my* needs,' he
bit out, his finger instinctively touching the velvety
smoothness of Simon's cheek, 'when they quite
clearly come bottom on your list of priorities!'
Simon began to whinge, and wordlessly Cormack
handed his son back to Triss, who managed to
soothe him.

She tried to act normally. She settled Simon in
his high chair, put his bib on and spooned his meal
into him, all the while making the funny little noises
which always made him giggle so much.

But all the time she was horribly aware of the
accusing blue stare which her ex-lover directed at
her. She had seen passion on Cormack's face
before, yes—many times—but never of this mag-
nitude or this intensity. And this was not passion
which was inspired by love or lust either, but a
strong, barely contained emotion which had more
to do with hate.

The tension and the bitterness emanating from
him were almost palpable, and perhaps that disturbed even Cormack, for he stood up suddenly,
his hands deep in the pockets of his trousers. He
strode over to the French doors which looked out
over the gardens and stood there, silent and un-
moving and very slightly menacing as he gazed
sightlessly at the blaze of yellow daffodils which
swayed in the breeze.

Triss finished Simon's meal with some yoghurt and fruit and he lapped it up greedily as she spooned it into his mouth.

'You *like* that, don't you, darling?' she cooed approvingly, then looked up to find that Cormack had silently turned and was watching them intently, as a cat might watch a defenceless little mouse just before it pounced on it.

'Raspberries?' he queried in surprise. 'You're giving him raspberries?'

He made it sound like arsenic! Triss thought. 'Yes, I am!' she said defensively. 'What's so odd about that?'

'Out of season and very expensive,' he observed.

Triss glared at him, resenting his judgmental tone and that critical look which was making his blue eyes glitter like sapphires. 'Right on both counts.'

'So do you spoil him, Triss?' he asked. 'By giving him everything he wants? Perhaps to make up for him not having a father?'

Triss glared at him again. 'What if I do?'

He shrugged. 'At five months it scarcely matters. But I would have thought that as a basic rule for bringing up a child then giving him everything he wants might make him spoilt and ungrateful as he gets older—'

Triss rounded on him. 'You've only observed me with Simon for all of ten minutes!' she spluttered. 'So how *dare* you cast doubts on my ability to be a good mother?'

'I was just pointing out—'

'And what would *you* know about bringing up a child anyway?' she demanded, her words tumbling out furiously—like water spilling from a washing machine.

'Nothing at all!' he returned calmly, the muscle working frantically in his cheek the only indicator of his anger. 'Since you refused me the right to have any kind of say in Simon's upbringing! But no more, Triss,' he continued, with a fierce kind of determination. 'No more will you succeed in keeping me out of his life!'

She lifted her chin up and her eyes looked very bright and very green at that moment. But her proud look masked a feeling of fear. 'Are you trying to intimidate me, Cormack?'

Did he sense that she was close to breakdown? Was that why his voice softened as he shook his head? 'No, I'm not. What good could come of that? I intend to be totally up front with you, Triss. No games. No secrets. I shall tell you exactly what I want when it comes to Simon.'

'And if I refuse?'

'It'll make things far more difficult for everyone concerned if you do—yourself included.'

She shook her head helplessly. 'I just don't know how we're going to resolve this.'

He shrugged, and his voice became tinged with bitterness as he said, 'Then perhaps, for the first time in our relationship, we might try a little compromise. Just because our love affair is finished it doesn't mean we have to ruin Simon's life into the bargain, does it?'

His words made her feel like crying. Or rather, one word in particular did. 'Finished'. Their love affair was 'finished'.

This was all most peculiar. *She* was the one who was supposed to be feeling a sense of triumph right now—with Cormack the distressed and injured party. So why the role-reversal? And why did she feel so empty all of a sudden?

Had she been holding onto some vague little hope in her heart that the sight of Simon might make Cormack want to try and rekindle their romance?

Well, she could kiss that hope goodbye.

For, no matter how well he adapted to being a father, she must never lose sight of the fact that she no longer had any place in Cormack's life except as the mother of his child.

CHAPTER SIX

CORMACK shoved his hands deeper into the pockets
of his trousers as he subjected Triss to a moody
blue stare.

'I'm going now,' he told her.

Hope and disappointment warred inside her as
she wiped a trace of raspberry juice from one corner
of Simon's delectable rosebud mouth. *'Going?'* she
squeaked loudly.

His mouth twisted into a parody of a smile.
'Don't get carried away with excitement, sweetheart,' he drawled. He reached out his hand to
touch the top of Simon's dark head lingeringly, and
there was something almost wistful about the
gesture which tugged relentlessly at Triss's
heartstrings.

For the first time she got an inkling of just how
much she had wounded him by denying him his
child. Uncomfortably, she opened her mouth to tell
him so. 'Cormack—'

'I'm going into London to sort out a few things,'
he interrupted brutally. 'Like bringing my clothes
down here, and rescheduling a couple of meetings
I had lined up during the week.'

'Oh, please don't let *me* stand in the way of your
meetings,' said Triss sarcastically as the horrible

way he had spoken to her dissolved some of her feelings of guilt.

'I won't,' he returned with cutting emphasis. 'It's nothing to do with you.' He gave her a cold smile. 'I'm doing it for Simon. And I'll be back—have no doubt about that, Triss.'

'When?' she enquired baldly. She plonked Simon's favourite rattle onto his high-chair tray and followed Cormack out of the kitchen.

'Tonight.' His answer was just as blunt.

'*Tonight?*' Triss wrinkled up her nose, then gave him a pleading look, unable to stop her gaze from slowly roving over the length of that delicious body. How she wished that he would move those gorgeous legs out of her line of vision! They reminded her of things she would much rather forget—like her stupid and impetuous behaviour back at the cottage.

Had she *really* just fallen into bed with him again? How could she have done—especially after what had happened last time? She was seriously beginning to wonder if there was *any* hope for her where Cormack Casey was concerned.

'But why tonight?' she appealed. 'Wouldn't it be better to leave it until tomorrow, when we've all had a decent night's sleep?'

'Better for who?' he demanded, in a voice which had all the gritty texture and coldness of iron shavings. 'Certainly not for me, nor for Simon. It might be better for you, sure. Does it interfere with prior commitments, Triss? Maybe you've got a heavy date you can't break?'

'If you're going to continue insulting me by making completely spurious claims about my sex life, then—'

'Then what?' he interrupted unsmilingly. 'Then you'll attempt to behave even more ruthlessly towards me? What's next on your agenda, Triss? To grant me a fleeting glimpse of my son and then to take him right out of my life again?'

She shook her head, shocked—naïvely, perhaps—by the undisguised bitterness in his voice. 'Of course not.'

His mouth tightened into a forbidding line. 'But there's no "of course" about it, is there? You spent nine months carrying my child without even bothering to tell me, and when he was born you chose not to inform me of that either. Clearly you must hate me with a passion, Triss.'

His gaze was very steady, but unmistakable pain glinted in the azure eyes as he asked, 'Did I really treat you so badly that my behaviour warranted such callous treatment?'

He could be very persuasive—she had forgotten just how much. But she had not made those heart-breaking decisions about Simon for the good of her health. And while Cormack might now be playing the innocent, injured party with the kind of skill which could have guaranteed him a promising career as an actor it was vital that Triss did not forget what had started her out on this course of vengeance.

'Did I, Triss?' he asked softly, in a honeyed voice she could happily have drowned in. 'Treat you so badly?'

Her huge hazel eyes sparked green and gold, like fireworks at the end of a summer party. 'That's a question you have to ask yourself, Cormack,' she told him quietly. 'Not me.'

Their eyes met for a long moment before he gave her the benefit of one of his most winning smiles, and Triss almost reeled under its impact.

'Can I borrow your car?' he asked, with an unconsciously guileless look which could bring out the maternal instinct in the most hard-bitten and cynical career-woman. Triss knew this for a fact—she had witnessed it on countless occasions.

'What would you do if I said no?'

He moved closer. Close enough for Triss to be able to detect that enticingly masculine scent of lemon and spice which was all Cormack's own.

'I'd change your mind for you,' he informed her softly.

'I'd like to see you try!'

He smiled. 'That sounds awfully like an invitation to me, sweetheart. Want to put it to the test?'

That was just the trouble. She did. And yet she didn't. She knew damned well from that wickedly hungry look glinting in his blue eyes just what method he would employ to persuade her to lend him her car.

And if he kissed her now it might prove her complete undoing. She was only just recovering from the episode in bed at the cottage—and, frankly, she was surprised that Cormack had not mentioned it since they had been back. Not once.

Was that out of consideration for her feelings? Or because he was saving up the memory of her uninhibited sexual response to throw back in her face later?

His features were just a few tempting inches away.

'Well?' he murmured, on a throaty caress. 'Shall we?'

'No, thanks,' she gulped, and stepped back quickly, as if he had just produced a sword and had begun to brandish it.

She was treated to a mocking smile.

'Pity,' was all he murmured as he opened the door and stepped over the threshold, pausing just for a moment. 'Goodbye, sweetheart,' he said quietly. 'I'll be back later.'

'G-goodbye.'

Triss stumbled back into the kitchen to find that Simon was in the act of smearing yoghurt and raspberries all over the tray of his high chair, and that a good deal of it had made its way into his hair, his ears and all over his blue and white striped dungarees!

She automatically picked up a roll of kitchen paper, tore off a generous handful and began to wipe the yoghurt off, but her mind was miles away. She scarcely even noticed when Simon leaned forward to lay a trusting but sticky cheek on her breast, depositing a pink, raspberry-scented blob in the process.

The mind, she had decided a long, long time ago, was something that could be controlled through will alone. And Triss was an expert on the subject—she had certainly practised it enough times!

You could lock certain memories away so that they could not torture you with their sweet poignancy—and that was what Triss had forced herself to do during the long months of her pregnancy, when she had felt so isolated and so alone.

The subject of Cormack had been like a cream cake to a determined dieter—something to be avoided at all costs! She had bided her time and waited, determined to find the optimum time to inform him that he was a father.

And then she had blown it by leaping so eagerly into his arms today. So what on earth did that say about her? Or him?

Triss sighed as she plucked Simon out of his high chair and carried him upstairs for his bath, knowing that she was weakening. Knowing that she was allowing her thoughts to wander along normally forbidden paths.

And one question alone clamoured to be heard.

Just what had happened to her and Cormack along the way?

After that first, sun-dappled lunch in Cormack's favourite restaurant in Malibu, Triss went back to his beachside house with him, knowing that she fully intended to go to bed with him.

She should have felt intimidated. He was, after all, one of Hollywood's most eligible men, and he had certainly had more than his fair share of equally eligible girlfriends.

Not that Triss was in the habit of putting herself down, or anything. Far from it!

She was aware that the rest of the world rated her looks very highly even if she, along with many other top models, could see only the flaws and imperfections in her face and figure. She knew that mere beauty was fleeting and fame was a fickle mistress, and that because of this her future depended on something which could not be predicted.

In short, she was hopelessly insecure!

Many men—worthy, intelligent men—had attempted to seduce her in the past, but she had never been remotely tempted by any of them.

Up until now.

Over their simple Californian lunch they had swopped life stories immediately, as if eager to get them out of the way.

Neither of them had been particularly happy as children, but Cormack's upbringing had been the harshest by far. He was one of five children, the youngest by a good eleven years, and so, in effect, an only child.

When Cormack was growing up, his siblings had already left home, leaving them well clear of Joseph Casey, their father, and his long-standing love affair with the bottle.

When poor health finally took its toll and carried off Cormack's mother when the boy was just twelve, Joseph Casey found that he was finally beyond the criticism of another adult, and proceeded to take comfort in liquor more than ever before.

It was a frightening existence for a young boy. Cormack was blamed for everything. When Joseph was sacked from yet another job, it was Cormack's fault for being such a demanding child. When there was no money for food, Cormack was accused of eating it all. And with the accusations came physical violence, which became worse, not better, as Cormack grew from a boy into a fine figure of a man.

And it was the violence which finally convinced Cormack that he must break free.

At sixteen he ran away to Dublin, where he became lead singer with an unknown rock band whose fortunes were to change once the brilliantly acerbic Cormack Casey started penning their songs. In terms of popularity and sales, the band broke every record in Ireland before storming Europe and then, eventually, laying claim to the greatest musical prize of all—the United States.

Triss listened as Cormack explained all this, in his soft, lyrical Belfast accent, her eyes huge and rapt as she stared at him. 'Why on earth did you leave the band?' she questioned. 'When it was going so well.'

'It's a young man's game.' He smiled. 'For people who plan to wreck their health! Besides, I get more of a kick out of constructing make-believe characters for the movies. Now...' His intelligent blue eyes seared into her. 'Tell me about you.'

'I—' She looked up at him, her hazel eyes huge and bewildered as she realised that she actually *wanted* to pour her heart out.

Men had alternately tried to cajole or drag the story from her over the years, but she had always clammed up in her shame, obstinately determined to tell them nothing. The difference here was that there was something about the soft blueness of Cormack's eyes which just invited confidence.

But the habit of a lifetime was hard to break and Triss shook her head.

'Leave it, then,' he suggested, in a voice so soft and soothing it made Triss want to curl up and purr.

'I—I *want* to tell you,' she began hesitantly.

'Then tell, sweetheart.'

So she told him about growing up as the daughter of a woman so exquisitely lovely that her beauty had tainted her life for ever. A woman who had been unable to accept growing older, who had seen her only daughter as a threat rather than as someone to love.

'She loved my brother,' said Triss, taking a sip from her iced spritzer. 'He's a doctor and he's married now—to another doctor. They're both doing very well,' she added quietly.

'You don't mention a father in all this.' Cormack shot her a shrewd look.

She shrugged. 'That's because he wasn't around when I was growing up. He disappeared one day— quite literally, as it turns out—nobody has seen him for years.'

'What was he like?'

Triss shrugged her narrow shoulders again. 'He was a glamorous playboy who just happened to lose all his money, and when that happened he lost my mother too.'

'So how did you survive?'

Triss shuddered as her mind wandered back down forbidden pathways. 'Oh, there was never a shortage of suitable "escorts" for a woman who looked like my mother. For suitable, read rich,' she added, unaware of the cynicism which had briefly hardened her voice. But Cormack heard it, and frowned.

'She lived off men, basically,' explained Triss, in a forced voice which sounded shaky even to her own ears. 'She still does. Only as the years go by and her looks diminish, well, her standards drop accordingly. Consequently the men get more and more disgusting. She's...' Her voice tailed off in distress, but Cormack did not attempt the false comfort which would have rung so emptily in her ears. 'She's living in the South of France at the moment, with a man who made his fortune from manufacturing dog biscuits.'

She blew her nose noisily and escaped to the powder room. When she came back, Cormack was settling the bill, and she looked at him gratefully.

'OK?' he queried, and she nodded. 'We can always have dessert at home, later,' he added, and to Triss's fury she found herself blushing.

Now they were driving back in Cormack's open-topped Aston Martin, with the sun glinting off the Pacific which dazzled in a sapphire haze beside them. Her long hair floated behind her like a bronze banner which gleamed as shinily as the paintwork of the racing-green car.

When he drew up outside the dazzling white house, he switched off the engine and turned to look at her, his eyes narrowed, his expression thoughtful as he took in her tense, hunched shoulders, her tightly clasped hands. To Cormack, her whole body language was yelling, Leave me alone!

'Changed your mind, sweetheart?' he enquired softly.

'About what?'

'Staying with me.'

'Would it matter if I had?' she asked him boldly.

He reached out a hand and freed a glossy tendril of hair the colour of cinnamon from where it clung to the full pout of her lips. 'Of course it would *matter*,' he answered softly. 'But not in the way you might be thinking.'

'You're a mind-reader, are you now, Mr Casey?'

He smiled, and it was the most irresistibly roguish smile that Triss had ever seen. 'I don't need to be,' he said simply. 'They say that the eyes are the windows to the soul, don't they? And yours are telling me everything I need to know right now, sweetheart.'

'Which is?'

'That you want me as much as I want you—'

Triss clapped her palms against her flaming cheeks. 'Cormack!' she protested. *'Don't!'*

'Don't what? Don't speak the truth?' he mused. 'But why ever not? Why stifle emotion with convention?'

Intrigued, she asked, 'And is that what I'm doing?'

'Sure it is. You want me to take you to bed, but now you're having second thoughts—thinking that we haven't known each other for very long. Or not knowing whether my intentions are...'

'Honourable?' she supplied, midway between laughter and indignation.

Humour danced in the bright blue eyes. 'Well, of course, I can't promise you marriage at this stage—'

'That wasn't what I meant!' she raged, wondering if she was not protesting a little *too* much.

'No? Then what did you mean?'

'Why don't you tell *me*?' she snapped, aware that she was sounding more and more petulant, but annoyingly unable to stop herself. 'Since you seem to be the self-appointed expert.'

'Oh, I am,' he murmured. 'I am indeed.' And all conversation ceased when he leaned forward and kissed her.

Triss had never believed the fictional kisses of books and films, which could have a woman swooning helplessly in a man's arms after just one touch of lip upon lip, but now she became the most fervent convert.

It was magic—like no other kiss she had ever had. So much so that she almost found herself wondering whether Cormack had slipped some powerful aphrodisiac into her drink at lunchtime—except that instinct told her he would have neither the need nor the inclination to do something as crass as that.

She felt giddy with the joy and the promise of that kiss—it felt as though little bubbles of happiness were exploding and fizzing around her veins. She felt abandonment wash over her like a tidal wave, and she began to moan against his mouth—and heard his own answering moan, which was tinged with more than a little desperation.

And when the kiss was finally over, and they had managed to tear their lips apart in order to drag some air into their tortured lungs, Triss found that his hand was beneath her thin white dress and resting proprietorially at the top of her naked thigh, stroking it beautifully.

And somehow her own hands had slipped luxuriatingly beneath the silk of his shirt and were splayed with equal possession over the velvety smoothness of his back.

His eyes looked as black as coal shipped directly from hell, and through his ragged breath he said something which must have been in Gaelic, for it was like no language she had heard before.

With what seemed a monumental effort, he took his hand away from the soft, silky skin of her inner thigh and levered himself as far away from her as possible—which was not easy, given the rather cramped intimacy of the Aston Martin.

'That wasn't fair,' he said, more to himself than to her. 'Shall I take you home now?'

It was like being woken up in the middle of the most delicious dream, and Triss stared at him with a look of exasperation on her face. 'No!' she responded, so indignantly that Cormack was unable to stop himself from smiling. 'I thought we were going to bed together.'

'Are you a virgin?' he demanded suddenly, his Irish accent sounding very distinctive.

She wondered how he had guessed. Had she kissed like an amateur? It did not occur to her to deny it. 'Y-yes,' she answered tentatively.

He smiled again, only this time it was like the sun coming out on Midsummer Day—bright and blinding—making every other smile seem hopelessly insignificant.

He lifted her hand to his mouth and kissed it gently, his eyes never leaving her face as he did so. 'Do you know something, Triss?' he murmured. 'I've never been a man for prayers, but I think you just answered mine in any case! Now, quick and decide. Am I taking you back home, or are you staying here? Either way I'm having breakfast with you tomorrow. And lunch. Supper too. So what do you say?'

Triss was hooked.

'Sounds like I'm staying,' she whispered, and let him lead her into his house.

First, for propriety's sake, he took her into a state-of-the-art kitchen where he made her scented jasmine tea. Then into his white bedroom—bare save for a simple futon on which he slept. The floorboards were made of pale, honey-coloured wood which gave off the softest sheen. White muslin covered the futon, and it billowed gauzily in the gentle breeze which blew in through the open window.

There was not even a single painting on any of the stark white walls, for art would have detracted from the living art which was right outside—a picture window filled with all the different blues thrown up by the sea and the sky.

'Now come here,' he whispered softly.

He took for ever to undress her, so by the time she lay naked in his arms all her shyness had flown and she was as eager for him as he was for her— indeed, of the two of them, he seemed capable of showing the most restraint.

And when it was over she cried because he had made it just perfect. He kissed her tears away and asked her to move in with him, and naturally she said yes.

Triss was due a long holiday, and so she took it straight away, and Cormack postponed his new film script so that they could spend some time together.

For the first few months it was the relationship she had always dreamed of. And more.

They had time and money on their hands, but most of all they had each other. They were living in a fairy-tale bubble which kept the rest of the world out, and Triss found herself wondering just how long it could last.

The bubble burst when Cormack reluctantly told her in bed one morning that he really *did* have to go into the studio to discuss his screenplay of a novel by an up-and-coming writer.

As he spoke, Triss felt enormously grateful for the acting skills which her modelling career had instilled in her.

She put on her brightest smile, then let her mouth drift slowly down his chest to the indentation of his belly, and he gave that helpless groan of surrender she so loved to hear.

For a while Triss played the dutiful housewife, aware that most of her day seemed to be spent waiting for Cormack to turn up. She had never been much of a cook, and she wasn't really inclined to learn. Why bother cooking something for Cormack which would invariably be spoiled because he never seemed to get home when he *said* he would?

When he *did* get home, he wanted to take her out—to restaurants and parties and films—which at first Triss enjoyed. But then she began to grow jealous of the attention which other people—especially women—gave him.

She found that she wanted to stay in their love-nest—to go back to the early days when they had only needed each other—safe from the temptations and distractions of the outside world.

But Cormack became restless with this stay-at-home life, particularly after one of the increasingly frequent visits from Brad Parfitt. Brad was his powerful and rather ruthless agent, who seemed afraid that the threat of domesticity would make Cormack's creativity shrivel up and die.

'I need to go out, sweetheart!' Cormack told her passionately. 'I need to see other people and the world. I'm a *writer*, Triss—and I need something to write about!'

She realised that she was now in a subservient role to Cormack. He refused to let her contribute to the household expenses while she was not working, so, in effect, she was living off him—and in that respect was she any different from her mother?

And then *her* agent began to call again, saying that people would not wait for ever to book her, that her face might not always be flavour of the month and that she really ought to start working again—capitalise on her assets while they were still in demand. Which meant travelling again.

Cormack didn't like it one bit.

'Why the hell can't you model here?' he demanded. 'In Hollywood?'

'Because I'm an *international* model,' answered Triss, unconsciously quoting her agent, word for word. 'And my looks are too European to appeal to Americans.'

He shot her a disbelieving look. 'And you believe that?' he asked incredulously. 'Why not let *me* ask around, find you something?'

'*No!*' Her response was swift and definite. 'I want to be independent, Cormack.'

'Then so be it.' He shrugged, but his voice carried a trace of unmistakable disquiet.

So Triss flew first to Paris, then to Rome. And it was in London that she saw the first of the newspaper items, tucked discreetly into the corner of the country's biggest gossip column. A picture showed Cormack with his arm resting lightly around the shoulders of a reed-thin girl with hair the colour of pale corn and a wistful smile as she gazed up at him, which gave her face a kind of dreamy look.

They had a fierce row about it on the phone that night, in which Triss interrogated him and he told her that the woman was an actress who would be starring in his film, and that she meant nothing to him. And also that, hey, he'd thought that their relationship was based on trust.

'Oh, it is, Cormack!' she sobbed. 'You know it is!'

'Then what the hell is this all about, sweetheart?'

'It's just that I *miss* you! And I want to be there.'

'Then be here,' he told her simply. 'Catch the next plane out.'

'I can't. You know I can't—this job is going to last another week.'

His Irish accent sounded matter-of-fact. 'Then if you can't or won't change the situation you must accept it, Triss.' A distant babble of voices hummed like bees on a summer's day in the background.

'What's that noise?' demanded Triss, hating herself for doing it.

'Just some people. Brad. Louie. Nick. Jenna. We're going out to catch that new film.' His voice lowered. 'I miss you, sweetheart.'

'I miss you too,' she gulped.

But the seeds of suspicion were sown in a mind which provided fertile growing conditions for more suspicion as each day passed. The times when they *were* together took on—for Triss, anyway—the sensation of standing on quicksand.

They were no longer completely at ease. Sometimes she found that they were eyeing each other warily across the room, like two predators sizing up the competition. She was aware that their relationship seemed to be shifting beneath the surface—and that there was nothing she could do to stop it.

She was in Milan when her mother kindly sent her the article with the accompanying photograph. It showed Cormack out sailing in the company of a group from the studio, with a tiny brunette peeping adoringly at him from underneath a thick, glossy fringe, and Triss experienced an extraordinary feeling which could almost have been described as relief.

Because, in a way, she had been freed from the prison of loving a man as much as she loved Cormack. Now she could stop hoping and stop trusting because, in the end, it turned out that he was just the same as every other man.

Triss had only her own experiences to base her life on. She had grown up in a world where money ruled, where infidelity was as normal as apple pie and where promises were made to be broken.

She went back to Malibu and packed her bags, then left Cormack a letter saying that she had made a mistake. And she returned to London.

He tried to contact her, but she refused to take his calls and ignored his letters. But she was unable to ignore him when he turned up on her doorstep one day, straight off the early-morning flight.

The change in him was frightening. He seemed so distant, so remote. Like a stranger—only worse than a stranger. And his eyes were as coldly sharp as razor-blades. What was more, he made no attempt to touch her. Perhaps, if he had, the whole scenario might have been different. But there again, what was the point of continuing their relationship if the overpowering sexual attraction between them was the only thing which sustained it?

His voice was tinged with ice as he said, quite calmly, 'Do you intend to continue this elaborate charade of hysterical behaviour, Triss, or are you willing to sit down and discuss the situation like an adult?'

And, naturally, the insult with which he had begun his question evoked a similarly insulting response in Triss.

'Get out of my flat, you no-good philanderer!' she snapped, and was shocked and mortified when he turned around without another word and did exactly that.

She missed him so much that it was as if half of her had gone with him, and she sent him a tentative letter, saying that perhaps one day they could be friends.

She received a cold little note by return of post saying that no, they couldn't—because one of the pre-requisites of friendship was the existence of trust.

And that Triss had not yet learned the meaning of trust...

CHAPTER SEVEN

WHILE she waited for Cormack to return Triss bathed Simon, who was showing absolutely no sign of tiredness. She played peep-bo with him, and his delighted little chuckles rang out around the sumptuous art-deco bathroom.

He was an absolutely gorgeous baby, she thought, with a surge of fierce maternal pride, as she bundled him up in a big fluffy towel. And Lola had said that he had been as good as gold with her and Geraint.

Triss found herself wondering what Simon himself thought of Cormack. Did he have any inkling at all that the tall, dark Irishman was, in fact, his father? Were babies born with the instinctive equipment to detect their birth parents?

She let Simon lie on the floor and kick his chubby little legs. Then she dressed him in his Disney pyjamas and settled him down in his cot, putting on the teddy-bear mobile which played nursery rhymes—which Triss always sang along to, even though she had not been born with the most tuneful voice in the world!

Then she fed him, savouring those blissful moments of having him clamped to her breast and glugging contentedly. She was still breastfeeding first thing in the morning and last thing at night, and Simon seemed to be accepting this now, although it had been difficult at first.

She hadn't wanted to wean him quite so early, but a look at her bank statement last month had convinced her that she could no longer afford the luxury of continuing to play the role of full-time mummy.

She had spent most of her savings on this house, which was her investment for Simon's future. The rest she had been living off. She had not worked since discovering that she was carrying Cormack's baby. She had been too plagued by morning sickness even to consider working at the beginning, and then, when the pregnancy had firmly established itself, she had done everything in her power to look after herself.

She had been mentally and physically exhausted after her run-ins with Cormack, and so she had quite deliberately nurtured her baby in the womb, taking as much rest as she could.

It was almost seven by the time Simon's eyelids drooped and he fell fast asleep, his thumb firmly in his mouth. Triss crept out of the room feeling gritty and sticky and uncomfortable, her cheeks reddening as she remembered the reason why.

Well, she would wash every trace of Cormack Casey from her body, and maybe after that she might feel able to confront him with some degree of calmness this evening.

She showered and washed her hair, then dressed in a pair of black leggings and slouch-socks. She put a huge black sweater over the top then looked at herself critically in the mirror.

Hell, but she looked pale! And her shorn hair made her eyes look unnaturally huge in her face. In fact, she was about as far removed from the woman Cormack had fallen for as it was possible to be. And feminine pride meant that this fact rankled more than a little—especially to someone whose whole career had been based on looking beautiful.

Should she wear some make-up? Perhaps rub a little blusher into those deadly white cheeks?

She decided against it. If she made herself up, it might look as though she had seduction in mind— when really all she wanted to do was talk to him, establish some kind of practical framework whereby Cormack could have some contact with his son while he was growing up.

In the end she compromised and put on a pair of large, beautifully worked silver earrings, which Cormack had bought for her in a shop in Greenwich, where they had once spent a blissful weekend. They were studded with small polished ovals of amber and, while they were not the most precious things she owned, they were certainly her favourite—though she didn't stop to examine too closely her motives for wearing them now.

She checked on Simon, then went downstairs. She was just deliberating on whether or not she ought to concoct some kind of supper—even though she did not have the slightest bit of appetite—when the telephone rang. She snatched the receiver up as though it were a lifeline.

'Hello?'

'Triss?'

Her first disappointed thought was that it was not Cormack. Triss recognised the voice immediately—it was Martha, her sister-in-law and dearest friend. A qualified obstetrician, she had cared for Triss throughout her pregnancy, and had delivered Simon with great emotion.

'Martha!' Triss exclaimed, and then said immediately, 'Cormack has rung you, hasn't he?'

'Yes, he has.' For once Martha sounded cross. *Very* cross. 'Oh, *Triss*—how *could* you?'

'How could I what?'

'Don't play the innocent with me, young lady! You know darned well what I'm talking about! He was furious to discover that Simon's existence had been kept a secret from him. Triss, you told me—'

Triss found herself flushing guiltily. 'Yes, I know...'

But Martha would not be deflected; Triss had never heard her beloved sister-in-law sound quite so angry. 'You told me that Cormack had said he never wanted to see you again. You told me that he wanted nothing to do with your pregnancy, nor with your child! And now he informs me that he knew nothing of your pregnancy. Absolutely *nothing*.' She exhaled an exasperated breath. 'When I think of all the times I wanted to contact him— only you made me promise not to on pain of death!'

'Martha . . .' Triss gulped with genuine remorse. 'I'm so sorry. Blame my hormones. Or blame my infantile inability to accept that, while my relationship with Cormack was doomed, it didn't mean that I had the right to deny him our son. I'm only beginning to realise that now.'

'I felt such a heel when he rang,' said Martha sadly. 'And such a fool. Because I liked Cormack, *really* liked him. So did Michael. We still do.'

'If it's any comfort to you, then I feel a heel too,' said Triss miserably.

'Darling, you should have confided in me.'

'You would have told him.'

'Ye-es,' agreed Martha slowly. 'But would that have been so very awful, Triss? He would have stood by you, supported you—'

'And I could not have taken that impartial kind of support from Cormack!' declared Triss hotly. 'Not at that stage! Not when I was still so much in love with him and the relationship was over.'

'Triss, are you quite sure it was over?' quizzed Martha gently.

'He started having a relationship with someone else!' sobbed Triss. 'How sure can you get?'

'Maybe he—'

'Maybe *nothing*! Because during that relationship he and I met at a party and tumbled into bed together, and that was how Simon was conceived! And if he was capable of committing infidelity while he was in a relationship with someone else, then what the hell was he doing all the time he was with *me*?'

Martha's voice sounded worried. 'Triss—'

But Triss raged on, unable to stop. 'Remember all those photos taken of him with adoring women while I was on the other side of the world?' she demanded.

'You mean the ones your mother went to so much trouble to make sure you would see?' enquired Martha caustically.

'And I'm grateful to her!' declared Triss wildly. 'Otherwise how else would I have known?'

'Triss—'

'At the time he tried to convince me that they meant nothing, Martha! But how could I ever be sure? That's the main reason I left him—because I could not stand living with the jealousy he made me feel!'

All the anger and the bitterness came bubbling out, like poison spilling out of a witch's cauldron. 'He hurt me, Martha! He hurt me so badly that I honestly thought I couldn't keep going—but I *had* to keep going, for Simon's sake. And the only thing which kept me going was the thought that one day I would hurt him back.'

'An eye for an eye, you mean?' queried her sister-in-law acidly.

'If you like.'

'Revenge is a very negative act, you know, Triss—'

'So is betrayal.'

'Triss, have you actually talked to him about it?'

'No.'

'Listen...' Martha sighed. 'He's going to be staying with you, isn't he?'

'Did he tell you that?'

Martha laughed. 'No—ever since I've become a consultant obstetrician I've developed powers of clairvoyancy! Of course he told me—how else would I know? Come on, Triss. I know everything about the whole situation is a little heavy, but try to lighten up a little, for goodness' sake! Not to mention for your sake—and Simon's—and—dare I mention it?—Cormack's too!'

Triss managed a small smile. 'Sorry. I know I'm Gloom of the Year at the moment! What were you going to say?'

'Just that we could come over—if you like. For lunch on Sunday, if it's a fine day. It might help to ease the atmosphere between you. And if other people are around—well, you can't just go at one another hammer and tongs, now, can you?'

It sounded like a good idea. 'I'll call you,' said Triss. 'Listen, I have to go—there's someone at the door and it's probably Cormack.'

'Go, then—and good luck,' said Martha. 'And *ring* me! OK?'

'I will. Bye!'

Triss felt as nervous as a child going to school for the first time as she pulled open the door.

Cormack was standing there looking absolutely scrumptious, and Triss felt her heart sinking with despair. He had no right to look that good, she thought to herself. No right at all!

He had changed from the black leather and was dressed now with an almost quiet conservatism—which, conversely, only made him look all the more elementally sexy: pristine white jeans and a slub-silk shirt in palest blue, with a much darker blue sweater knotted casually around his neck. From his finger swung a soft navy jacket.

His blue eyes glinted, although Triss could not be sure if it was with devilment or irritation.

'Finished?' he queried softly, and Triss realised to her horror that she had been ogling him like a groupie!

'Come in!' she said hastily.

He entered the hall with a thoughtful kind of dignity, as if he had not been there earlier that day, and Triss felt unaccountably nervous. She noticed, too, that he carried a brown leather holdall, presumably containing enough clothes for…how long?

'Have you eaten?' she babbled.

'No.' He put the holdall down by the coat stand and hung up his jacket. 'Have you?'

She shook her head. 'I could cook us something…'

'Or we could ring out for a pizza or a curry?' he suggested.

Triss shook her head again. She thought of the forced inactivity while they waited for the food to arrive—and wait they would certainly have to. Delivery companies always had tremendous difficulty finding houses on the estate, since each one was tucked away so discreetly.

'I'd rather cook,' she told him. 'There's plenty of food. Come through to the kitchen—it's this way.'

'I know,' he reminded her gravely. 'I was here earlier, remember?'

'Yes, of course!'

In the kitchen, Triss felt momentarily nonplussed, wondering if her hands would stop trembling enough for her to be able to chop up anything at all. 'What do you want to eat?'

'Don't mind. Heat up a pizza or something.'

But that was the last thing she wanted to do. If she provided him with instant food, then it would leave all that time dragging interminably while it heated up. And they would either be left swopping polite, meaningless pleasantries, as they were now, or hurling bitter recriminations at each other across the room.

At least if she cooked she could keep herself busy—wouldn't have to stare into those beautiful blue eyes which reminded her with a pang that was almost unbearable of just what she had lost.

She stared at him rather helplessly. 'Would you like some wine?'

'Please. Want me to open it?'

She nodded, fished out the best red she could find in the rack and handed it over to him.

He extracted the cork and half filled the two glasses she had pushed across the counter towards him. There was a slightly awkward moment when she lifted her glass to toast him—more out of habit than anything else.

His mouth curved into a sardonic line. 'What would you like to drink to, Triss?' he enquired mockingly. 'To secrets?'

'Or to betrayal?' she countered sweetly.

'And how am I supposed to have betrayed you?'

'There is no *supposed* about it!' she snapped, taking a huge slug of wine which made her feel better immediately. 'You *did* betray me, Cormack!'

'You mean that I made love to you when I was involved with another woman?'

'Damned right I do!'

'I see. You don't think that if I betrayed anyone it was Helga? She was, after all, the woman I was having a relationship with at the time. Not you.'

Triss stared at him in shocked disbelief. 'I don't believe you just said that.'

'Don't you? Do you think that you are solely entitled to my loyalty, Triss? Even though I had not seen you or heard from you then for almost two years?'

To her astonishment, he settled himself on one of the stools, took a sip of wine and contemplated his glass thoughtfully. When he looked up again his blue gaze was quite steady.

'It might be easier,' he told her calmly, 'if you were able to see the incident within the context of the wider issues at stake.'

'How *dare* you patronise me?' Triss slammed her glass down on the counter and wine slopped into a claret puddle on the white marble. 'And what the hell was *that* remark supposed to mean? Are you trying to blind me with Hollywood psycho-babble now, Cormack? When the bottom line is that you were in a relationship with some—'

'Helga was not *some* anything!' he interrupted immediately, his voice gritty and abrasive.

'*Oh?* You're defending her honour now, are you?' Triss finally snapped, and all the bitterness and jealousy which had eaten away at her for so long suddenly erupted like a sore left to fester.

'Of course I'm defending her honour,' he responded, with a quiet dignity which reminded Triss of why she had loved him so much—though his words absolutely appalled her.

'Y-you are?'

'Why on earth not? Or would you expect me to treat a woman I respected badly?'

'Then why didn't you marry her?' she cried angrily. 'If she was so bloody marvellous!'

He drew in a deep breath. 'Because I was not in love with her—' their eyes met for a long, tense moment '—the way I was in love with you.'

Triss noticed his use of the past tense and could have wept. She drank some more wine instead.

'Helga was the innocent party in the whole affair,' he said. 'You and I had been apart for almost two years when I began dating her. So tell me, was that such a heinous crime, Triss—to want to see someone else?

'You had quite steadfastly and adamantly refused to discuss what had gone wrong between us,' he continued, his blue eyes blazing. 'Our relationship was over—you'd made that quite clear.

And, yes, I found your suggestion that we could one day be "friends" an insulting one.'

She began to mop up the spilt wine. 'You aren't one of these modern men who believe in a civilised ending to an affair, then?'

'In theory, perhaps. In practice, not always—no. And certainly not to an affair which had been as passionate and as intense as ours.'

'That didn't mean that you had to leap into bed with the first woman who came along!' she accused him.

'I did *not*,' he emphasised, with barely concealed impatience, ' "leap into bed with the first woman who came along." Nor the second, nor the third. Et cetera. Women throw themselves at me every day—and frankly I find it a turn-off. I always have done. I am not promiscuous, Triss, and I never have been. And what is more you do me a great disservice in judging me by the same standard as some of the more questionable escorts of your mother's—'

'Just you leave my mother out of it!' she yelled.

To her surprise, he backed down immediately, holding the palms of his hands up in a placatory fashion. 'Very well, we'll leave your mother out of it.' He threw her a frankly questioning stare. 'But did you really expect me to forsake all other women for the rest of my life? To carry your memory around engraved on my heart?'

'Don't be sarcastic with *me*, Cormack Casey!' she warned him.

'Then don't be so bloody unrealistic with me!' he snapped. 'Just because you and I had split up—that did not mean I intended to remain celibate for the rest of my life! Or was that what you expected, Triss?'

The certain knowledge that he had slept with another woman was like a knife being plunged through her heart. Oh, she knew that it wasn't logical, and she certainly knew that it wasn't even fair—but that did not stop the sickening images from swimming before her eyes.

'Stop it,' he told her gently, as something in her face must have told him her thoughts. 'It's over. It meant—'

'Don't you *dare* tell me it meant nothing!' she yelled. 'Helga Summers happens to be one of the world's most beautiful actresses. So how can it not have meant something?'

He gave her a reproving look. 'Her beauty has nothing to do with it. And I was not about to say that it meant nothing. Of course it meant some-thing—all relationships do. But that does not mean that it meant the same to me as what I shared with you—'

'*Don't!*' She tried to clap her hands over her ears but he wouldn't let her.

'You *will* hear me out, Triss Alexander,' he told her grimly. 'For once in your life you will face up to facts and not bloody conjecture!' He pushed her down onto a stool just before her legs gave way.

She raised her head to find him studying her with a concerned and narrow-eyed scrutiny. 'Oh, what's the point?' she demanded wearily.

'The point is that our lives are irrevocably linked—through Simon—whether you like it or not. And we need to discuss topics which have been swept under the carpet for much too long.'

'Like?'

'Like the night of his conception, for example.'

'No—'

'*Yes!*'

Triss closed her eyes but that made it even worse, for the memories clicked sharply into place—like a camera which had just been focused properly.

She tried to recall just how she had felt at the time, and the conflicting waves of misery and elation came sweeping back to swamp her...

CHAPTER EIGHT

WHEN Triss had split up with Cormack, she had been determined not to become a wet blanket as so many women did when love failed to live up to their expectations.

She did not need a *man* to define her! she decided. And she had lots and lots of good things going for her—a successful career, her youth and her vitality.

She had only ever rented apartments before, and so the first thing she did when she arrived back from Malibu, with all her belongings in tow, was to begin looking around London in earnest for a place to call her own. More importantly, a place which would have no connection whatsoever with her erstwhile lover.

After a great deal of searching she found exactly what she was looking for. It was relatively small—especially if she compared it with what she had shared with Cormack, so she made an effort not to—only a two-room flat plus kitchen and bathroom, but its beauty was its position. It had an uninterrupted view over Regent's Park which made Triss feel as though she was living in the middle of the country instead of minutes from the centre of London.

She flung herself into decorating it with a passion and soon it was completed in the soft, restful shades of blue and cream she loved so much.

So she had her home and her work. The only area of life which she seemed to be missing out on was a busy social calendar. And this was simply unacceptable—at least according to Triss's brother Michael and his wife Martha.

Michael and Martha were doctors who lived on the outskirts of London, and they both nagged Triss to go out with a gentle persistence which gradually won her round to their way of thinking.

Maybe they were right. After all, she couldn't sit around like a hermit moping for Cormack for the rest of her life, could she?

'So what are you going to do about it?' Michael demanded one day.

'I will go to the very next party I'm invited to,' Triss told her brother solemnly.

'Promise?'

'Cross my heart.'

As it happened, the next party she was invited to was on New Year's Eve. Triss drove across London for afternoon tea with Martha and Michael, and they quizzed her about the location.

'It's near Brighton—an enormous white house overlooking the Downs,' Triss told them.

'And whose party is it?' queried Michael.

'You remember Alastair McDavid?'

'The photographer?'

'Mmm. He's just finished decorating the house and says he wants to invite every person he's ever liked!'

'So why you?' joked Michael, and was rewarded with a long-suffering glare from his sister.

'Sounds glittering,' remarked Martha.

'Hope so,' said Triss—and she meant it. She intended to have a good time tonight—even if it killed her!

She pulled out all the stops and dressed up for the party as she had not dressed up for a long time.

She dug out a glittering gold-beaded mini-dress and some outrageous thigh-high gold leather boots, sprinkled with silver stars, which she had bought on her last trip to Paris.

She decided that she would look like a Christmas tree if she left her hair loose, so she piled it into an elaborate chignon and found earrings which were a cascade of silver stars and matched the detail on her boots.

Like most models, she tended to play her make-up down when she went out more to give her skin a rest than for any other reason. But tonight she needed the make-up—needed it as a mask to hide behind.

She applied blusher and a provocative brush of scarlet gloss on her lips, and used a dusting of gold powder on her eyelids which made her eyes look huge and dazzling—like a cat's caught in the headlights of a car.

When she had finished she blinked bemusedly at herself in the mirror—because the creature staring back at her was the catwalk Triss: highly glamorous and more than a little distant. It was, she knew, a look which threatened all but the most confident men.

Good! she thought gleefully. She needed any social comeback to be gradual, and the last thing she wanted tonight was unwanted men homing in on her with seduction in mind.

She shuddered a little, wondering if she would ever be able to contemplate the thought of intimacy with a man who wasn't Cormack without feeling violently ill.

It was a wild late December night when she started off with a wind-chill factor which promised snow and the usual gloomy predictions from the weatherman, and advice to people not to leave their homes unless their journey was 'absolutely necessary'.

Well, Triss had decided that her journey *was* absolutely necessary. Necessary to her sanity, that was! She was still recovering from the forced jollity of Christmas, when she had missed Cormack quite unbearably and had spent too much time scanning the post every morning for a card that never came.

The party *was* glittering, as predicted, though Triss saw few faces she recognised—which was a relief. People she knew were still fascinated by her affair with Cormack, and always seemed to want a blow-by-blow account of why it had floundered. And she still found that too painful to relate.

She moved around the room in her glittery gold dress with unconscious grace, sipping her champagne and nodding politely as people spoke to her—until the unbelievable happened and Cormack walked into the room.

And Triss wondered whether she would ever be able to formulate a sentence again.

What on earth was *Cormack* doing *here*?

He looked directly across the room at her and Triss stared back, her mouth opening to form a dazed 'O' shape. It was so corny she could have screamed—if she hadn't been so busy feasting her eyes on him, and marvelling at how wonderful he looked.

So why was it, she wondered, that *he* could wear black jeans and a black cashmere sweater and look an absolute knockout? Like sex on legs. While the other men who had obviously gone to loads of trouble and were dressed in formal evening attire—well, they just faded into the background in comparison!

Oh, it's hopeless, Triss told herself fiercely. Absolutely hopeless. You are *not* to compare him with the other men, and you are not to talk to him either.

So they both played an elaborate charade. Triss pretended to ignore him, spiritedly entering into conversation with everyone or rather *anyone* other than the tall, brooding man with the black hair who was attracting every available woman to his side, like wasps around a jam-jar.

Triss tried her best not to glower as the women hovered around him unashamedly. Although she did have to admit that Cormack *appeared*, at least, to be totally unmoved by all their attentions. He just stood there on the opposite side of the room to her, looking so cool and aloof, like some dark, beautiful statue.

And it was not until supper was being served that she actually spoke to him. Or rather he spoke to her.

She was standing at the end of the line, trying to decide if she would be able to eat *anything* without choking on it, when she heard a familiar deep voice behind her.

'So who are you trying to impress tonight, sweet-heart?' came that distinctive Irish accent.

Triss whirled round and her heart began to pound uncomfortably against her ribcage as she registered how close he was. 'Well, it certainly isn't *you*!'

He merely shrugged. 'Oh, I guessed *that* all right. For if you were you wouldn't have slapped two tons of make-up on your face like that. And what in the name of God did you put it on with, Beatrice? A trowel?'

Triss drew her shoulders back and gave him an icily sarcastic smile. 'That's what I like to hear, Cormack—you entering wholeheartedly into the party spirit—I *don't* think! More like a lead balloon!'

In a frozen silence they glared at one another, but their animosity only seemed to enhance the charge of sexual tension which crackled between them like electricity.

He drew in a deep breath, like a person facing a particularly unpleasant endurance test. 'So how are you, Beatrice?' he asked heavily.

What was he expecting to hear? That she was as miserable as sin? That she was missing him like mad? That she despaired of ever being able to feel a tiny fraction of affection for another man?

'I'm fine!' answered Triss, a determinedly bright smile on her face. 'Absolutely fine!'

He nodded. 'Good,' he said, the word sounding as if it was being dragged painfully from him.

The silence which followed was unendurable. Close up, Triss found herself wanting to run her fingertips over the shadowed curve of that strong jawline. She felt her hands actually begin to tremble with the urge to do so. And she knew she had to get away before he began to suspect how she still felt about him.

'Excuse me,' she told him shakily, 'but I really must get myself some food.'

'Of course,' he answered formally, and she noticed for the first time how pale he looked. 'I could use a drink myself.' And he turned swiftly on his heel and left the room without another word.

After that, the party was ruined for Triss. Although she had planned to stay the night, for two pins she would have left right then. But the snow which had been nothing more than a choc-olate-box flurry when she had arrived had been pelting down in thick and steady earnest as the party had progressed.

At one point four of the men, including Cormack, went outside to investigate the weather conditions.

'We're snowed in!' Alastair announced gleefully on their return, and the party erupted into cheers—although the only thing that Triss registered was Cormack's darkly glowering face as he stood behind Alastair, his blue-black hair peppered with snowflakes.

The music was turned up, glasses refilled and a real festive feeling took over as people got down to some serious dancing before counting the New Year in.

But for Triss it was nothing more than an ordeal to be got through, and by a quarter to midnight she couldn't take any more. Unobtrusively, she sneaked over to Alastair and asked him to allot her a room as far away from the madding crowd as possible.

'Stay and see midnight in at least?' he pleaded gently, but Triss shook her head.

'I won't, thanks all the same, Alastair,' she told him quietly. 'I have a splitting headache—I'm no fun for anyone tonight.'

Once safely in her room, she heaved a huge sigh of relief, took off every scrap of make-up, untied her hair and brushed her teeth.

I am not going to do anything as predictable as crying into my pillow, she told herself firmly as she pulled her nightshirt over her head. In the past two years I have cried more than enough tears over Cormack Casey, thank you very much!

She took a book from her overnight bag and settled down in bed to read, because although she had made up her mind not to fall to pieces she was realistic enough to know that there would be little sleep for her tonight—not with Cormack settled in bed just yards away.

With someone else? she wondered briefly, but blocked the thought immediately because that was just *too* painful to contemplate.

She listened to the distant chimes of midnight and the singing of 'Auld Lang Syne,' and then the sounds of people gradually settling down for the night.

By four o'clock the house was completely silent, and Triss was still wide awake.

She slid out of bed, put her head outside the door and listened, but there was not a sound to be heard. Telling herself that a drink would help her sleep, she padded downstairs to the kitchen and poured herself a glass of milk. She sipped it standing by the sink, looking out of the window, noting that the snow had finally stopped falling and that the sky was now clearing. In the distance, the silvery light of the moon was becoming more visible by the minute as the snow-clouds scudded away like jet planes.

After she had drunk her milk, she washed the glass out and stood it on the drainer to dry, and made her way back upstairs.

And there, at the top of the landing, by the wide window-ledge, stood a motionless figure.

Triss took in those shadowed, sharply hewn features, saw the moonlight playing on the muscular definition of his bare skin, and her heart gave a helpless lurch.

'Cormack?' she whispered, half reluctantly, as if words might break the enchantment of seeing him there, like that, clad in nothing but a pair of jeans and looking so ridiculously *approachable*.

'Hello, Triss.' His voice was soft, and something in the way he smiled at her made it impossible to do anything other than go over and stand beside him.

'What are you doing?'

'Watching the moon,' he told her, but he wasn't—he was watching her. He lifted a hand to indicate her free-flowing hair and her scrubbed face. 'That's much better,' he observed.

She certainly wasn't looking for his approval, and yet the warmth in his voice made her reluctant to say so. She turned to face him. 'Is it?'

'Mmm. You look so beautiful when your face is bare.'

And you look so beautiful when your chest is bare, she thought, though she said nothing about that either.

As he watched her intently he reached his hand out towards her arm, and one forefinger lightly stroked the cuff of the thigh-length shirt she wore. 'And this is mine, isn't it?' he asked, a note of surprise in his voice.

In the darkness, Triss found herself blushing. What a complete and utter give-away! Fancy parading around the house at the dead of night wearing this old dress-shirt of his, which she had refused to give up—like a child hanging onto a much treasured security blanket. 'You gave it to me, remember?'

'Did I?' he teased. 'You borrowed it for a party, as I recall, and never gave it back!'

'Yes,' she gulped, overcome with nostalgia.

The silence which followed should have been awkward, but it was not; it was comforting and reassuring and gloriously, gloriously familiar. They stood side by side, watching the full silvery radiance of the moon which turned the snowy landscape into a fairy-tale picture of silver and white.

Triss recalled how they had used to watch the moon in Malibu too, in silence—just like this. Was Cormack remembering that as well? she wondered.

She felt the speed of her heartbeat pick up and begin to pound in her ears, until she was certain that he *must* be able to hear it too.

'Triss?' he said suddenly, quite urgently.

She turned to look into eyes which gleamed with dark, sensual promise and she began to tremble.

Afterwards she would never be quite sure who made the first move. All she knew was that somehow she was in his arms again. He was holding her tightly and she was holding him back as though she could never bear to let him go—and nothing else in the world seemed to matter.

They just stood like that for ages. After a while he took her hand and brought it to his lips and kissed the palm slowly, lingeringly, a question narrowing his darkened eyes. And Triss must have answered it mutely, for he silently led her down the corridor to what was obviously his room.

She made no protest as he quietly closed the door behind them. He did not put the light on, but there was light enough from the moon, and he reached out his hand and moved it slowly down the side of her face, like a blind man reading his way by touch alone.

Her eyes were wide with her own question as he took her once again into his arms and stared down at her in a way which made her begin to quiver helplessly.

'Cormack,' she whispered. 'Should we be doing this?'

'I can't not do it,' he answered simply. 'Unless you tell me to.'

She shook her head. 'That isn't fair!' she protested. 'You know I can't do that.'

'Well, then.' He smiled, but it was a smile tinged with sadness as he drew her down onto the bed and began to kiss her with all the restrained and sensual exploration that she remembered from the very first time he had made love to her.

Except that this time she knew what to expect, knew that the act of lovemaking itself would surpass all her wildest dreams, and she returned his kiss willingly, eagerly, until she heard the deep sigh of pleasure which meant that he was finding restraint very difficult indeed.

His hands were actually trembling as they peeled the shirt from her body, and she lay naked and bathed in silver moonlight as she watched him kick off his jeans, doing her best not to squirm with impatience until he was back beside her on the bed.

Just before he entered her he told her that he loved her, but Triss scarcely heard him—her body was crying out with so much need for the fusion with his.

It was quite unlike any other time they had been intimate together, and Triss was moved beyond words by the surprisingly slow, erotic coupling which took her to unimagined heights. Cormack was more tender than she had ever known him, and she felt as though he was piercing the very heart of her as her kiss-muffled cries echoed softly around the room.

And I love him too, she thought. *Still.* More than I have allowed myself to admit. I must tell him . . .

But in the end she told him nothing—not straight after they had made love, anyway. She was too dazed. Too elated. Too smugly complacent as she lay tangled with him amid the rumpled sheets and contemplated a future which was suddenly bright— a future which included Cormack.

They were drifting in and out of an easy, warm sleep, when somewhere in the distance Triss heard the ringing of a telephone which went on and on and on. Oh, why doesn't somebody answer it? she wondered half impatiently, and then the ringing stopped abruptly.

Somebody had, she thought with relief.

Through the mists of sleep she heard a rapping on the bedroom door, and Cormack stirred beside her, his finger and thumb moving instinctively to tantalise her nipple.

'*Oh,*' she sighed, and shifted her body towards his, and he gave a low laugh as he ran his hand possessively over her bottom.

'Cor-*mack*!' yelled a voice from outside the door. 'Phone!'

'Go away!' growled Cormack as he let his mouth drift lazily over Triss's breast. 'I'm busy!'

'It's urgent!' persisted the voice. 'It's Helga!'

Triss felt him freeze, and then he sat up. And the expression in his eyes told her everything she needed to know. For written in their lapis lazuli depths she could read despair. And guilt.

And Triss knew that whoever Helga was—Cormack was involved with her.

He didn't say a word to her as he swung his legs over the side of the bed and began pulling on his jeans. He didn't have to, for self-condemnation had etched an unbearable strain on his features.

By the door he paused, turned round and said, in a voice of almost unendurable tension, 'Triss?'

But she shook her head, clapped her hands fiercely over her ears like a child and buried her face in the pillow.

And only when she heard the door click behind him did she sit up, with tears streaming down her cheeks, and begin to plan her escape.

CHAPTER NINE

TRISS closed her eyes and forced the memories to recede, and when she opened them again she was momentarily disconcerted to find herself sitting in her cosy bleached-oak kitchen at St Fiacre's—miles and months away from snowy Brighton—with Cormack watching her thoughtfully.

'We never resolved that night together, did we, Triss?'

She swallowed the last of her wine. 'What's to resolve?'

'Plenty.'

'No!' She refilled her glass and saw him frown.

'You should eat something,' he observed.

'Go to hell, Cormack Casey! When I need a nanny I'll look for one—and I certainly won't choose a philandering—'

'Triss! For God's sake, *stop* all this!'

'Give me one good reason why I should!' she yelled.

'Simon,' he answered simply.

'That isn't fair,' she said bitterly. 'That's emotional blackmail!'

He gave her a long, steady look. 'Don't talk to me about emotional blackmail, Triss,' he said quietly. 'Because in those particular stakes you played the trump card by keeping my son a secret from me. If that isn't emotional blackmail, then I don't know what is.'

'Yes, I did!' she declared. 'And if you want to know why I did it then I'll tell you! I did it because it made me feel good. I enjoyed the planning of it *and* the thought of it! I *enjoyed* carrying the secret around with me, if you must know!'

And it had only stopped being enjoyable when she had been confronted with Cormack again, and had realised the enormity of her actions in keeping his own flesh and blood hidden from him. And now, instead of feeling triumphant about her act of revenge, she felt mean and low and nasty.

But she was not going to tell him that. Why should she? Telling him would only reveal her dangerous vulnerability where he was concerned. And besides, he had shown very little in the way of considerate feelings towards *her*.

'And all because of Helga?' he asked sadly.

'Don't you *dare* make it sound as though Helga was just some casual acquaintance of yours! You were having an affair with her, weren't you?'

'I *had* been—'

'So what was she doing ringing you up at six in the morning on New Year's Day? That does not sound like the behaviour of an ex-lover to me.'

Cormack sighed. 'Would you give me the opportunity to explain?'

Triss bit her lip—hard. Anything to stop that threatening and give-away wobble in her voice from developing. 'Is there any point?' She scowled.

'I thought that we'd already decided that, yes, for Simon's sake, *of course* there is a point.' His eyes narrowed as they took in the fact that she was perched tensely on the very edge of one of the high stools by the breakfast bar. 'You don't look comfortable there, Triss.'

'I'm not.'

'Then why don't we take our wine into the sitting room? Have you any cheese?'

Triss nodded. 'In the fridge.' She thought about how ungracious she was being and resolved to make more of an effort. 'Why? Are you hungry?'

'Ravenous,' he admitted, then shot her a deliberately lazy smile. '*Something* must have given me an appetite...'

Triss felt her cheeks burn and closed her eyes in horror. It was hard to imagine now what had taken place this afternoon within minutes of their meeting.

And did he *have* to remind her of it? There she had been, just seconds earlier, foolishly vowing to be nice to him, when clearly he had no compunction about embarrassing *her*.

'Why mention that?' she cried. 'And why now?'

'Why not?' he challenged. 'We've been studiously avoiding the subject ever since it happened. Is that something *else* which is to be brushed underneath the carpet, Triss? Ignored as though it never happened?'

'It shouldn't have happened!'

'Maybe not,' he admitted, and Triss felt her face crumple at his easy agreement. She took another huge slug of wine so that he wouldn't see.

'But it *did* happen,' he continued, and went to open the refrigerator door and peered inside. 'So maybe we need to ask ourselves why.'

'Why?' Triss echoed.

'Mmm.' His blue eyes were very candid as he turned to look at her over his shoulder. 'Why, after everything that's happened between us, did we still fall into bed with each other today?'

'I would have thought that was fairly obvious,' answered Triss repressively. 'It's one of the baser human instincts and it's known as lust.'

He didn't answer her, just pulled out a plastic box and began to take various lumps of cheese out. 'Oh, go and sit down, Triss,' he told her impatiently. 'I'll bring this in when I'm ready.'

She topped up her glass and took it into the sitting room and lit the lamps, so that the room looked warm and peachy and inviting. It was cold enough for a fire, too...

Minutes later, she had the beginnings of a blaze crackling in the grate. She sat down in one of the armchairs and must have dozed off, for when she opened her eyes again it was to find Cormack towering over her, a tray in his hands with a bowl of something steaming on it.

She sat up. 'That smells good. What is it?'

'Soup. I found a carton in the fridge. And there's a melted-cheese sandwich too.'

'My favourite,' she said automatically, pleased in spite of everything, and yet acutely aware that she was straying into dangerous emotional waters here.

'I know,' he said abruptly. 'I'll go and get mine.'

They ate their supper in silence, and when they had finished Cormack took the plates out. She could hear him stacking the dishwasher.

She had forgotten his scrupulous fairness about the allocation of household chores, and yet he managed to knock up a simple meal without losing one scrap of the blatant masculinity which was so much part of his appeal.

When he returned, he sat down on the rug in front of the fire and looked at her. 'You say you don't want an explanation about that night—'

'I don't!' she put in quickly.

'Is that because you are determined to think the worst of me?' he probed quietly. 'Does it make you feel better to imagine that I behaved like some brainless stud?'

'Not really.' And that's a *lie*, Triss Alexander, said the voice of her conscience.

'I think it does,' he disagreed perceptively. 'Believing the worst of me enables you to keep your hatred of me alive, doesn't it, Triss?'

'No.'

'*Yes!*' His voice sounded angry now, and his blue eyes were spitting fire. 'Don't you think that after everything we shared together you at least owe me the courtesy of listening to an explanation?'

'I'm listening.'

He seemed to be choosing his words very carefully, for it took him several moments to continue. 'I met Helga a long time after we split up—'

'How very convenient for you.'

'*Triss!*' he thundered savagely. 'You are testing my patience to the extreme! Now, are you going to shut up and listen to what I have to say—or am I going to be forced to assert my mastery?'

Her heart raced and her mouth dried as her body responded automatically to his words. 'Y-you w-wouldn't d-dare!'

'Wouldn't I?' Suddenly he smiled and the anger was gone—although the sexual promise wasn't. 'No, you're right—I wouldn't.' There was a pause. 'As I said, I met Helga nearly two years after you and I split up—'

'And in all that time you never once contacted me!' she accused him, aware even as the words tumbled out that she was giving herself away.

'And neither did you,' he retorted softly, 'contact me.'

'But *you* were the one who said you didn't want to be friends—'

'Not didn't *want* to be,' he corrected her. 'I just felt we couldn't be. That our somewhat tempestuous relationship was not a particularly sound basis for friendship. And I assumed that the relationship was dead since neither of us had been able to make it work.'

He shook his dark head. 'I stayed alone for a long time, but when Helga came along she was...'

He shrugged and spread out the palms of his hands rather helplessly.

'Tell me,' she said, though the words choked her.

'Easy, I guess.' And then he saw her expression and shook his head again. 'Oh, not in the commonly used sense. I mean that she was undemanding, uncomplicated—'

'The opposite to me, in fact?'

He did not flinch under her accusing stare. 'If you like. I certainly wasn't looking for a replica of the intensity I had shared with you, Triss.'

'So what happened?' she demanded. 'It sounds as though in Helga you found your dream woman.'

He regarded her critically. 'In theory, perhaps she was. She never answered me back the way you do. And she didn't have a jealous bone in her body.'

'So why no happy ever after?' enquired Triss caustically. 'Or did your night of sex with me put paid to all that?'

'You can be such a little bitch,' he told her softly, and something in his eyes warned her that she really *was* stretching his patience just that little bit too far. 'I'm trying to tell it like it *was*, Triss—not how I would have liked it to be.'

And quite what he meant by that Triss didn't know—but judging by the look on his face now was not the time to ask him.

'So what happened?'

'Nothing actually *happened*. We just drifted apart, I guess, so gradually that our meetings became less and less frequent. Helga never actually lived with me, and she was based in Paris—'

'Paris again,' interjected Triss bitterly, thinking of how they had met. She stared at him, not even bothering to disguise the jealousy in her eyes. She had always thought of Paris as *their* city.

'Paris again,' he agreed, and his face was sombre. 'It was a totally different relationship from the one I had shared with you. When she was away I never actually *missed* her—not in the way I missed you.' He smiled. 'And Helga wasn't in love with me either. She always said that she wanted to marry another German. And she has. I'm godfather to their baby, as a matter of fact.'

'I see,' said Triss rather faintly. *Godfather?* Which meant that not only must Helga have the highest regard for Cormack, but her husband must too. What a manipulative Irish rogue he was! 'Carry on,' she instructed primly, 'with your story.'

His face was reflective. 'I hadn't seen Helga since October. She'd gone to visit her parents in Germany over Christmas.'

'And you?' she asked. 'What did you do over that Christmas?'

'I stayed home.'

'Alone?'

'Yep.'

Triss's eyes widened. 'But *why*? You must have had millions of invitations.'

He smiled, and it was like the sun coming out. 'Not millions, Triss. Some.'

'But you didn't go out?'

'I chose not to.'

'And New Year's Eve?'

He turned away and poured himself a second glass of wine, so that his face was hidden from her. 'The New Year's Eve party was just a spur-of-the-moment thing.'

'I see.'

He shook his dark head. 'No, that's just the trouble—I don't think you *do* see, Triss. When I walked into that party, I knew I had got it all wrong and that nothing had changed. That there was still this overwhelming passion which burned deep inside me.' He challenged her with a piercing blue gaze. 'And in you, too, however reluctantly.'

'So you took me to bed, knowing—'

'You make it sound like an intellectual decision,' he objected. 'Which it was not.'

She ignored the interruption. 'Knowing that you were still involved with Helga.'

'Knowing that I was on the periphery of involvement,' he amended. 'That everything between Helga and me had changed. It was over. It had been over for months.'

'Had it?'

His gaze was unwavering. 'Absolutely. She knew it and I knew it—it was just that neither of us had actually got around to putting it into words. So, while perhaps *technically* I should not have been with you that night, in my heart it felt *morally* right—and that remained the important thing.' Although I knew that you would not feel the same,' he added sombrely. 'But, oh, Triss, it *was* right!'

She set her mouth into an obstinate line. 'Isn't that just a way of justifying your behaviour?' she questioned. 'If it feels good then it must be right?'

'I don't know,' he admitted eventually. 'But all I can tell you is that it *did* feel good. And it *did* feel right. You know it did. And my son was conceived as a result of it.' His face darkened and he added bitterly, 'Or so I now discover.'

She found that her hands were trembling uncontrollably, so that she had to knit them together in a clasp in order to still them. 'Well, just what did you expect?' she demanded.

'I expected you to tell me,' he said simply, 'that I was going to become a father. Was that not my right, Triss?'

'And you think that slaking your lust for one night gives you rights, do you?'

He put his glass down with a white-knuckled hand. 'If I had simply chosen to "slake my lust",' he bit out, 'then I would have chosen someone a lot more uncomplicated than *you* to do it with! Someone, moreover, who was not carrying around a load of excess emotional baggage! Don't make the situation any worse than it already is, Triss, by defining what happened between us that night in terms of mere lust!

'And tell me,' he continued relentlessly, his voice tinged with bitterness, 'did your primitive form of revenge make you feel really good? Isn't that what revenge is supposed to do?'

She thought about his questions carefully. 'Of course it's supposed to make you feel good—there is a sense of getting even when you embark on revenge—but ...'

His eyes were very watchful. 'But?'

'As to whether it has actually succeeded in making me feel good...then, no. Not now, it doesn't.'

'And before?'

She resented the tone of his questioning, as though everything were *that* simple. As though he were the angel in all this and she the big, bad devil.

'Yes, I suppose it *did* make me feel good for a while—although that was some time in coming after the initial bitterness. When Helga's call woke us up that New Year's morning, I couldn't believe that you could make love to me when you were still involved with someone else. Quite apart from what it seemed to say about your attitude towards me, as a woman, it seemed to belittle what we had shared before.

'I went back to London, nursing my hurt pride.' And her badly wounded heart of course, but there was no need for Cormack to know *that*. 'And a few weeks later discovered I was pregnant.'

'Were you scared?' he asked with soft perception.

His expression was too intense for her to do anything other than tell him the truth. 'I was absolutely petrified.'

'Then why the hell didn't you *tell* me?'

She gave a hollow little laugh. 'Tell *you*?' She shook her head, as though not believing that he could be quite so dense. 'Cormack, you were the last person in the world I even wanted to *think* about, let alone speak to! I didn't allow myself to consider you. Simon had become *my* baby—and mine alone.'

'So that's why you went into hiding? Why you instructed Michael and Martha to keep your whereabouts secret?'

'You could have found me if you had really wanted to!' she accused him, finally admitting to the pain she had felt when he had not come looking for her.

'Do you really think that I am the kind of man to force himself on a woman when she has shown every sign of not wanting me?' he drawled.

'Isn't that what you're doing right now?' she challenged. 'By staying here?'

'Oh, no.' He gave a cold, cynical laugh. 'The difference is that I am no longer concerned with what *you* want, Triss. My concern now is for my son—and *his* wants. His needs too. You have denied him a father through an emotion as shallow as a fit of pique—simply because you were jealous of another woman.'

Triss scarcely recognised her own shaky voice as she said, 'This has more to do with respect than jealousy.'

'Well, if it's about respect, then why don't you show me a little?' he queried gravely.

'And how do I do that?'

He gave her an odd smile. 'By marrying me, perhaps?'

CHAPTER TEN

TRISS turned to look at Cormack as though he had just taken leave of his senses.

What bitter-sweet irony, she thought, that he should at last have uttered the words she had once longed to hear. And what a pity that it should be in such unconventional and unsettling circumstances.

'*Marry* you?'

'Is that such a bizarre request, Triss?'

'In view of the contempt which you obviously feel for me, then I would say yes, it is.'

'But I notice that you didn't automatically reject the suggestion out of hand,' he mused.

Triss shook her head. 'That's because I'm intelligent enough to see that perhaps marriage does have something to recommend it—in our case. But that doesn't mean I'm going to agree to it.'

'Why not?' he enquired coolly.

'Because, while I recognise that the advantages to Simon of having both parents around would be huge, I think that they are outweighed by one fundamental disadvantage.'

'Which is?'

'That we find it impossible to exist in anything *resembling* a state of harmony.'

'But we did once,' he reminded her. 'Or have you forgotten that?'

Forgotten it? She had every moment of it etched indelibly on her mind! She ran her hand distractedly through her hair, realising that with all the planning and excitement and dread of the last few weeks she had not bothered to have it cut.

'That was a long time ago, Cormack—'

'It's a little over three years, Triss—hardly a lifetime.'

'It is when you've had a baby,' she whispered, and saw from the pained expression which clouded his eyes that she had wounded him when she had not intended to.

'That much has changed,' he conceded.

'And more too!' she cried passionately. 'We were young then—and in love...' Her voice tailed away dispiritedly as her mind registered how much it hurt to talk of love always in the past tense.

'Whereas now we're both old and cynical?'

'That's a bit how I feel tonight, yes,' she admitted, and stretched her arms high above her head in an attempt to ease some of the awful tension in her neck. 'Old and cynical.'

'Me too. So do you want to show me my room?' His blue eyes glittered as he noted the hectic colour which immediately stained her cheeks. 'It might do us both some good if we were to sleep on it. Don't you think?'

'Y-yes,' she agreed nervously. 'I'll take you up there now.'

'Thanks.' He rose to his feet, his whole manner one of detachment, his face betraying nothing other than mild curiosity.

Her knees felt as weak as a schoolgirl's as he followed her up the oak-banistered staircase.

She had mentally earmarked the room she was going to give him earlier, when he had gone away to collect his clothes. It wasn't the biggest room in the house, nor the best—in fact just about the only thing it had going for it as far as Triss was concerned was that it was the furthest away from her own!

She pushed open the door. 'There are towels there, and a bathroom just down the corridor,' she babbled. 'And I've left—'

'Where does Simon sleep?' he demanded suddenly.

She had known he was going to ask. Had been expecting it and yet dreading it. Simon all rosy with innocent sleep was gorgeous enough to break your heart in any case—but was she strong enough to cope with Cormack filling the role of adoring father, as she knew he would?

'In—here,' she croaked as she led him to the nursery, which was next door to her own room.

He pushed the door open and walked noiselessly across the thick pale blue carpet to where Simon lay, and for a moment he was distracted—not by the sight of his sleeping son, but by the crib he slept in.

He touched the carved shiny wood almost wonderingly. 'Where on earth did you get this?' he demanded, though his voice was little more than a whisper in order not to wake Simon.

'It's a long story,' she told him softly.

'Tell me.'

She told him falteringly.

She had seen the old-fashioned crib made from ancient dark wood and had ordered it, impulsively, on a shopping trip in New York. It had been in the window of a small furniture shop so cleverly tucked away in a back-street that just finding it had seemed to Triss like fate! She had been pregnant at the time, and emotional enough to tell the dealer that her baby's father was Irish and that he had gone away.

The wood was engraved with lines of mystical long-forgotten Gaelic poetry, and whimsical representations of leprechauns and shillelaghs and other, more obscure Irish objects of which Triss had no knowledge.

It was nostalgic almost to the point of being corny, but Triss had adored it on sight.

It had been, or so the dealer had told her, a testament to a much loved Irish childhood—built by an Irish father for a son born in America, so far away from home.

At great cost Triss had had the cot shipped back to England, and it had not been until he wrote to her, later, that Triss had discovered that the dealer himself had built the crib. He had signed off his letter with the promise that the crib would bring the baby's father back to her.

Triss had not believed it at the time, stuffing the letter to the back of a drawer and dismissing the words as those of a man whose vision was coloured by sentiment.

And yet the sight of the crib, dark and solid and comforting, had sown the seeds of an idea that keeping Simon a secret from his father for ever would not only damage the boy but also her own peace of mind for evermore.

Cormack nodded thoughtfully as she came to the end of her story, then turned his attention to his son, as though he had been saving the best bit for last.

Simon was sleeping, and had somehow managed to wriggle himself around so that he was the wrong way up in the crib, with his bottom pushed up against the headboard.

His thick black hair was ruffled, and he was dressed in a blue sleeping-suit dotted with Disney characters. His little security blanket was rumpled up beside his hand, while his duvet was nowhere near him.

Triss reached down over the crib and covered him with the duvet. She tucked him in and then automatically bent down to plant a soft kiss on his scented hair.

The movement did not waken him, but it must have disturbed him very slightly, for he stirred and kicked his legs a little until he found his thumb and stuck it into his mouth with a small sigh of pleasure.

Triss sneaked a look at Cormack, unprepared for the look of raw emotion on his face.

When you had lived with someone—even only for a year—you imagined that you had witnessed every emotion they were capable of expressing.

But not this one. Suddenly he looked like a stranger to her.

'Cormack?' she whispered tentatively. 'What is it?'

'Oh, Triss,' he sighed, and the note of anguish in his voice entered her heart like a knife-wound. 'How did we ever let this whole damn mess happen?'

She shook her head, too close to tears to want to answer him. She put her finger over her lips and crept silently from the room, and Cormack followed her.

Outside, she hesitated and said, 'Goodnight, then.' But he shook his dark head decisively and reached for her, and she allowed him to pull her into his arms.

What was she thinking—she *allowed* him? She felt so empty that she wanted him to do this, to lower his head to hers and to...

He kissed her slowly, thoroughly, and just that first touch was enough to overload every sensual pathway in her body completely.

Without thinking, she entwined her arms sensually around his neck and kissed him back, full and passionately on the mouth, and their lips parted at exactly the same moment, as if governed by the same instinct.

The kiss went on and on. And no matter how many times Cormack kissed her, Triss thought despairingly, he could always extract this same trembling sense of wonder from her, as though it were the first time all over again.

She felt the almost imperceptible change in his body as desire began to make itself felt, and some tiny trace of self-preservation began to slow her down.

For all their sakes—but most importantly for *Simon's* sake—Triss sensed that this time, at least, she must not give in to the demands of her body.

With an effort she pulled away and shook her head.

'No?' he queried.

'No.' She dragged in a breath of air.

'You didn't say no this afternoon.'

'That was different.' This afternoon she had been too consumed by hunger to be able to stop. 'I hadn't told you about Simon then.'

'No. You hadn't.' His mouth tightened. 'God— what do you *do* to me, Triss?' he demanded hotly. 'When you finally *did* tell me about Simon, about deliberately keeping him from me, I vowed that I would never lay another finger on you—never touch you again, no matter how much I was tempted to.'

'I know that,' she told him quietly.

'How?'

Triss shrugged. 'I knew that your sense of outrage at my duplicity would turn you off.'

He gave a bitter laugh. 'And in theory it should. Only somehow it doesn't work like that, does it, Triss? I not only find that my principles fly out of the window when I'm confronted by that luscious body of yours, but I'm prepared to compromise them even further by asking you to marry me!'

Triss shuddered. For in that one short, cynical speech he had made his feelings for her crystal-clear. How on earth could she marry him when he could talk to her like that? It didn't sound as though he had even the slightest regard for her as a person— although that was not really the point.

The point was that he was attracted to her against his will, and clearly resented the fact. And plainly he would never love her in the way that she still, she realised, loved him. Completely and without reservation.

So if she went ahead with what was essentially a marriage of convenience, then she would have to accept it for what it was. Because it would cause continued heartbreak if she found herself longing for an emotional commitment he was unable to give her.

She needed to sleep on it. To go over and over it in her mind. She did not want to be swayed or influenced by Cormack's delicious lovemaking into making a decision which could ultimately harm her, or Simon.

'I think we're both tired and emotionally fraught,' she told him, her green-gold eyes glittering in her white face. 'I know that I certainly am. We both need sleep and a chance to think things over. So goodnight, Cormack—I'll see you in the morning.'

Quite instinctively she reached up and kissed him on the cheek, and the gesture momentarily startled them both.

It was those small intimacies which were the most evocative, she thought as she showered before sliding into her satin pyjamas. The hugs and the small kisses and the reassuring little squeezes of the hand—those were the things which brought back memories of how close they had once been. And those were the memories which broke her heart.

Because the sex between them was superb and always would be superb. It was almost as if their bodies had been programmed to react to one another in the most mind-blowing way. But that unique chemical reaction was nothing to do with the sound foundations on which most people built their relationships—like love and respect.

Cormack was right, was her last waking thought. How on earth had they ever got themselves into this terrible mess?

To her surprise, Triss slept like a log, and when Simon woke her at six the following morning she had decided to do the best thing for her baby and approach their problems with a positive attitude.

Because babies were perceptive, and if she was going to start moping around the place then it wasn't exactly going to do Simon any good! Or herself, come to that.

She went about her normal routine with a resolutely cheerful air.

She changed Simon and then brought him into her bed with her for his early-morning feed, unbuttoning her scarlet satin pyjamas and latching him onto her breast. It was a moment of pure peace, and she loved this quiet time alone with her son, with just the sound of the birds trilling outside her window in the spring sunshine.

He was glugging away quite contentedly when a slight movement caught her attention, and she glanced up to find Cormack watching them, a look of rapt preoccupation on his face.

He was dressed in nothing but a pair of black silk boxer shorts which left very little to the imagination. From a distance she could observe him almost neutrally in this partially clothed state, in a way which she had been unable to yesterday, when they were in bed together.

Physically, he was as close to perfection as you could get. Broad shoulders and a finely muscled torso with narrow hips and strong, long legs. His chin was darkly shadowed, as it always was first thing in the morning, and it gave him a devilishly sexy look.

His eyes were narrowed, and there was such a look of *wonderment* on his face that Triss knew she did not have the heart to exclude him from this most intimate part of motherhood. She had excluded him from enough already.

'Come in,' she coaxed softly, marvelling at the transformation in him. Normally, just the merest glimpse of her breasts would have had his gaze raking over her with hungry anticipation. But now the expression in his eyes was soft, admiring and full of frank regard—though Triss would have bet her last dollar that if she were to put Simon back down in his crib then the look of hunger would be back in force!

He came to sit on the edge of the bed, looking gloriously unselfconscious in nothing but the silk boxer shorts, and Triss found herself wishing that she had asked him to get dressed before inviting him in!

'I didn't realise you were still feeding him,' he murmured questioningly.

'Only last thing at night and first thing in the morning.' She sighed, then said fervently, 'I hate giving it up.'

'Then why do it?'

She gave him a long look as she unhooked the baby and transferred him to the opposite breast. 'Because I'll probably go back to work soon—in some capacity—'

'*Work?*' he interrupted in a horrified voice, as if she had just broached the idea of opening up a brothel! 'Do you *want* to go back to work?'

She shook her head. 'Not really, no. I seem to have got modelling right out of my system.'

'Then why even think of it?'

'Because I need to support us,' she told him evenly. 'I need—'

'I'll give you all the money you need to stop you from having to go out to work,' he told her, his mouth tightening with suppressed anger. He shrugged broad, tense shoulders. 'Though maybe that was your sole reason for introducing me to my son, Triss? So that I could slip into the role of financial provider?'

'I don't want your rotten, stinking money, Cormack Casey!' she spat back at him proudly, and Simon lifted his head up, momentarily startled, before resuming his blissful glugging.

'It might not be what you *want*, sweetheart,' he declared, a half-smile threatening to curve his mouth as he took in her furious expression, 'but maybe it's what you need if it stops you farming out Simon to some child-minder!'

'*Oh!*' Simon had dozed off, so Triss gently eased him away from her, winded him, then put him into Cormack's arms. 'Only a *man* would have the nerve to use such an emotive phrase as "farming out" in connection with childcare! Millions of women go out to work every day and leave their babies—and those babies are thriving! And do you *really* think I would have someone sub-standard looking after my own son?'

He grimaced, and had the grace to look repentant. 'I'm sorry,' he said. 'Point taken and noted.'

Triss, who had been ready to launch into another animated defence of working mothers, quickly shut her mouth, the wind completely taken out of her sails by his apology.

'What shall I do with him now?' asked Cormack softly, glancing down at the warm, sleeping bundle in his arms.

'You could put him down to sleep while I shower and dress,' she suggested. 'Then we can all have breakfast together, if you like.'

'Do I have to put him down?' he queried. 'Couldn't he sleep like this for a while?'

Triss looked taken aback. 'Of course he can—that's if you don't mind?'

'Mind? I can't think of anything I'd rather do.' Then he grinned. 'We—ll, on *second* thoughts...'

And Triss found herself blushing as their eyes met.

That was how she left them, with Cormack holding the baby in the classic rocking position. Now *that* was one for the family album, she thought wistfully.

She took her jeans, shirt and underwear into the bathroom with her, since she did not want to get dressed in front of Cormack—and she didn't want to disturb him and Simon by asking him to leave either.

When she had dressed, Triss went and rescued him, taking the baby from him even though he made a half-serious sound of protest.

'We'll be down in the kitchen,' she told him. 'What would you like for breakfast?' she asked, and then wished she hadn't, for in the early days she had asked him that very question and the answer had always been the same—'*You!*'

The brief clouding of his eyes told her that he had remembered too, but the careless smile which followed drove all other thoughts from Triss's mind.

'What does Simon have?' he murmured.

'I thought I'd give him scrambled eggs this morning,' she told him, feeling strangely shy. Something seemed to have happened between the two of them, and some of the old ease and magic was back. And she liked it. She liked it *very* much.

Cormack gave a roguish smile. 'Then I'll have the same as Simon, please.'

Triss went down and put Simon in his high chair, only her hands were shaking so much that she could barely crack the eggs into the bowl. As it was, some of the mixture plopped onto the shiny linoleum floor, and Triss moved to the sink to find a sponge to mop it up with.

She was just rinsing out the sponge under the tap when Simon leaned right over his tray at such a precarious angle that Triss was certain he was going to go hurtling to the floor.

'Simon!' she yelled, and rushed from the sink towards the high chair, not seeing the egg white where it lay in an innocently transparent pool.

Her foot went from under her as it collided with the sticky mess and Triss was caught off balance, too startled to have the presence of mind to put her hand out to save herself.

Her last thought before she hit the floor was her baby—nothing must happen to her baby.

'Cormack!' she called out, in a thin, reedy voice. 'Oh, please . . . Cormack . . .'

And then the whole world went black.

CHAPTER ELEVEN

WHEN Triss came to she was lying down. Not on the kitchen floor, but stretched out on one of the sofas in the sitting room with Cormack hovering over her, his ashen, worried face barely recognisable.

At the sight of her eyelashes fluttering open he heaved a huge sigh of relief.

'Triss! Thank God! Oh, thank God!'

'Wh-where's Simon?' came her automatic response.

'In his pram. Outside.'

'Outside *where*?' she demanded in alarm. She tried to sit up, but with a firm, decisive hand he stopped her.

'Just there. Look.' He pointed out through the window. 'In the sunshine. Babies need fresh air. He's fine.' He knitted his black brows together furiously and a look of sweet concern came over his face. 'But it isn't Simon I'm worried about—it's you! Darling, how's your head?'

Darling? Triss wondered if hearing things was a well-known side-effect of banging your head. 'What happened?'

'You slipped on the kitchen floor. You must have spilt something—'

'Egg,' she put in, as if in a trance, and saw him frown at her rather dreamy response.

'You were only out a couple of minutes,' he continued, his gaze scanning her face closely. 'But I called Michael and Martha immediately. Michael is on call at the hospital, but Martha is on her way over. She'll be here shortly. She's going to look after Simon while I take you to the hospital.'

'Hospital?' Triss protested. 'But I don't need to go to hospital!' She tried to sit up again, but waves of nausea washed over her and she slumped back against the pile of cushions which Cormack must have built up into a small mountain behind her head.

'Oh, yes, you do!' he retorted swiftly. 'Martha says that as you lost consciousness—'

'Only for a few seconds!' she pointed out.

'A few seconds or a few hours—either way, you still need an X-ray.'

'Rubbish!'

'Beatrice—' he began, and Triss could not remember seeing him look quite so stern. 'I am not playing games here. Now, either you allow me to take you to the hospital when your sister-in-law arrives or I call an ambulance and we go there right now, with sirens blaring and lights flashing and a very confused little baby into the bargain!'

Triss slumped back again, feeling weak and helpless but also oddly satisfied. She had been on her own with Simon for so long that she had forgotten what it was like to be able to lean on someone else for a change. And it was rather comforting, she realised, to have someone else to make the decisions—even if Cormack *did* tend towards the very bossy!

'OK?' he quizzed.

'OK,' she agreed, at the same time as the doorbell pealed out. Cormack hurried out of the room to answer it.

He returned minutes later with Martha, her sister-in-law, who rushed over to Triss's side, her worried expression clearing slightly when Triss managed a wide smile.

'Are you OK?' she demanded, her fingers swiftly moving to Triss's pulse.

'I'm fine.'

'Where's Simon?'

'In his pram outside,' answered Cormack. 'He needs some breakfast.'

'Right.' Martha nodded decisively.

'But *I* can give him his breakfast!' objected Triss on a pathetic little wail. 'And I don't want to go to the wretched hospital either!'

Martha merely looked up and said serenely, 'Cormack?'

He bent down, scooped Triss up into his arms and carried her out to the car, and Triss could not help but notice the rather complacent smile on her sister-in-law's face as he buckled up her seat belt for her.

She felt dozy in the car, and she caught Cormack giving her a sharp, sideways glance before turning an even paler colour—something which Triss had not thought was physically possible.

'It should be *you* going to hospital!' she joked shakily.

'Keep talking,' he said grimly.

'Why?'

'Because Martha told me you weren't to sleep. Talk to me, Triss,' he implored.

'About?'

'About anything. About what is closest to your heart. Tell me about the day our son was born.'

It was the hardest thing she had ever had to do, but it served its purpose because it kept her talking. The words spilled out in an emotional torrent as she described the first sharp pain of labour which had speared at her womb in the middle of the night.

'He came a couple of weeks earlier than he was meant to,' she explained. 'I hadn't planned to be on my own.'

She saw the muscle which had begun to work convulsively in his left cheek.

'What did you do?'

'I rang Martha. She came straight away—which was loyalty beyond the call of duty, considering it was three in the morning! She kept me calm, kept me talking. Helped with my breathing. She...' Triss bit her lip.

'She what?'

'She wanted to ring you.'

His mouth thinned. 'But you wouldn't let her, I suppose?'

'No. And you must hate me for that. For denying you the opportunity of seeing your son born.' Was it the wooziness from knocking her head which gave

her the courage to voice her greatest fear? she wondered. Or was it simply that she had never known
Cormack quite so approachable, quite so open with
her?

'How could I hate you, Triss,' he answered
simply, 'when only a fool would fail to see why you
acted as you did?' He changed down a gear. 'We're
here,' he announced, with an unmistakable note of
relief in his voice.

Triss was disappointed that their arrival at the
hospital meant that their conversation was cut
short, but one fact remained in her mind, bright as
a new lightbulb—Cormack didn't hate her. He
didn't love her, no, but at least he didn't hate her.
So would that be foundation enough to start to re-
construct their relationship?

He insisted on carrying her all the way into the
accident and emergency department. Triss initially
felt mortified at such a brazen display of masculine
strength, and she was only slightly cheered by the
ill-disguised looks of admiration on the faces of
every woman they passed, with Cormack striding
along like a hero from a costume drama!

In A&E the nurse in charge said to him rather
reprimandingly, 'You really should have got a
wheelchair, sir!'

To which Cormack replied, 'But why bother? I
rather like this method of transport!'

And so did Triss—that was the trouble. In fact,
she really missed his warmth and strength when they
told her to lie down on some horrible cold, unyielding hospital trolley.

When the X-ray result came back, Triss was given the all-clear. The doctor handed Cormack a sheet of instructions on what abnormal signs to look for which might indicate that she needed to come back to hospital. 'And no emotional stress, please!' he warned perceptively as he picked up on some of the incredible tension which seemed to be flowing between the two of them.

Unfortunately, the doctor's instruction seemed to give Cormack the idea that he now had *carte blanche* to run Triss's life as he saw fit!

He banished her to bed on their return home and saw Martha off, and then proceeded to take full charge of Simon for the next two days—as if he had recently graduated with honours in childcare!

'How d'you know so much about babies?' Triss enquired as she spooned up the tomato soup he had brought her on a tray and watched while he constructed yet another pile of wooden bricks for Simon to swipe at with a chubby fist.

'How did you?' he countered, with a lazy smile.

'Instinct coupled with trial and error, I guess.'

'Same here,' he grinned. 'Though I discovered to my cost that Simon doesn't like having his hair washed!'

'Er—no,' agreed Triss, thinking that *that* was the understatement of the year!

'I think I ended up with more water on *me* than on him!'

Triss giggled at the thought of her successful scriptwriter being defeated by a little baby at bathtime, then drew herself up sharply.

What on earth was she thinking of? Cormack wasn't *her* scriptwriter. He wasn't her *anything*. He was Simon's father, nothing more, and obviously, being a regular sort of guy, he wanted *their* relationship to be as civilised as possible.

And so did she; she really did.

She was past the stage of seeing Cormack as Mr Evil and herself as the poor, betrayed victim. And she had more than exacted her revenge—a conclusion which brought her nothing in the way of satisfaction.

But the danger—for her, anyway—was that while Cormack remained here and continued to build a relationship with *her* as well as with Simon she might continue to weave all these pathetic little fantasies about him.

Sooner or later, the subject really must be addressed.

'Do you think we could ever possibly be friends?' she asked him suddenly.

'Yes,' he answered, much too quickly, and Triss felt her heart sink. Once he had loved her too passionately ever to be able to contemplate such a thing. And his complete reversal of opinion now must surely mean that his love for her had died?

'Cormack—' she began, but he shook his dark head decisively.

'Not now, Triss,' he told her gently. 'Let's wait until you're better before we discuss anything. Remember what the doctor said about emotional stress?'

It was his gentleness which disturbed her most. Cormack being *that* solicitous could mean only one thing. He wanted her to be fully recovered before he told her that his marriage proposal had been an ill-conceived idea, made on the spur of the moment.

But *she* had decided that she wanted him anyway—even if it was ridiculously one-sided. She had forgotten how golden life could be when he was around, and she could all too vividly picture the greyness of life without him.

But maybe Cormack was right. Maybe it *was* best if they tried their utmost to be friends. For surely enough water had now passed under the bridge for them to make that rational and adult progression? For Simon's sake.

'OK, then,' she agreed falteringly.

Two days later he called in her GP, who pronounced her fit and well, and Cormack saw the doctor out with a broad grin of satisfaction on his face.

He didn't return for a good ten minutes, and when he did he was still wearing that same, rather smug expression.

'I'm taking you out for lunch!' he announced.

'But—'

'Lola and Geraint are coming in to babysit. They're getting married next week, by the way! And we're invited.'

'They are? Oh, that's...that's...' It took one of the biggest efforts she had ever had to make for Triss's voice not to break down. 'Wonderful,' she finished lamely.

'Isn't it?'

'Do we *have* to go out for lunch?' she enquired, rather plaintively. Wouldn't it be better to get the old heave-ho in private?

'Yes,' he told her firmly. 'We do.'

She opened her mouth to object, saw that familiar look of determination and quickly shut it again.

At least if they were in a public place he might be extra, extra gentle with her. And sooner or later she was going to have to face the outside world again.

After these past few days, when she had lived exclusively with her child and the father of that child, she had felt cosseted and safe and secure. And now she felt as though he was cutting the lifeline which linked the three of them, and that soon she would be adrift, floating on a great big empty sea without her beloved Cormack.

'Where are we going?'

'I thought we'd try the restaurant here, on the estate. Then if you get tired it isn't too far to come back.'

And if she got stressed or tearful—likewise. The only trouble was that St Fiacre's exclusive grill-room would be full of rich, bored and beautiful women who would be eyeing up Cormack like vultures.

'Then I want to get changed first,' she told him firmly.

'You look just fine as you are.'

Yeah, sure, she thought as she cast a disparaging eye over her navy blue leggings and matching sweatshirt. She could just imagine the sort of reaction she would get walking into the restaurant wearing *these*!

Since Cormack had come back into her life, the most flattering outfit he had seen her in had been the rather uninspiring linen dress she had been wearing to meet him at the cottage. Apart from that, he had seen her in nothing that was remotely glamorous. Not unless you counted her satin pyjamas, of course, and Simon was always posseting his milk over those!

Well, if Cormack had decided that today was the day he was going to give her the push, then visually, at least, she was going to make him eat his heart out!

She went upstairs to her room and set to on her face with a vengeance, using every trick she had learnt during her modelling days to enhance her rather wan-looking appearance.

By the time she had finished, she looked all eyes—and Triss nodded with satisfaction. Cormack had always been a sucker for her eyes!

And how her hair had grown! Strands of it were now tickling the back of her long neck, and the few extra centimetres in length had softened her face and complemented the unconscious serenity which motherhood had given her.

She clambered into an outrageous lime-green leather mini-dress with zip-front and matching ankle boots, which had been given to her by one of Italy's most famous and avant-garde designers after she had modelled it for him. It was a one-off, and he had told her rather sensationally that he would never be able to bear seeing it on another woman because the dress was simply *her*.

Now, as Triss twirled in front of the mirror, she wasn't too sure. Oh, it looked superb, no question about *that*—because you needed a tall, lean and leggy look to get away with this kind of abbreviated garment. A model-girl look, to be precise. She just wasn't sure, she thought as she put on a pair of huge silver earrings studded with jade, whether the rather conservative St Fiacre's restaurant was quite ready for this kind of thing!

Cormack certainly wasn't. He blinked several times in quick succession when he saw her, and seemed lost for words for a moment, until he growled, 'Maybe we'll cancel that table, after all—and eat in.'

'Oh, no,' answered Triss tranquilly. 'I'm looking forward to it.'

'Hmm,' was his only response.

Lola and Geraint arrived, giggling happily and so openly in love that Triss could see that it was a real effort for them to keep their hands off each other.

'Geraint has moved in with me until we decide whether or not we're going to stay at St Fiacre's!' announced Lola.

'Which is rather convenient,' murmured Geraint, 'seeing as Dominic wants his house back!'

'So Dominic Dashwood is coming back for good, is he?' asked Cormack thoughtfully. 'Bang goes your peace and quiet then, Triss! The estate will be crawling with members of the Press.'

'Oh, no,' Triss disagreed, shaking her head. 'Security on the estate is tight, tight, *tight*—that's one of the main reasons I bought the house.'

'Is it, now?' queried Cormack, and threw Geraint a narrow-eyed look over the top of Triss's head.

Lola was bubbling over with excitement, and she kept waving her left hand around in a flamboyant arc, so that the whopping great solitaire on her finger cast rainbow rays in its path.

'Oh, it's gorgeous!' murmured Triss fervently, trying like mad to keep the envy out of her voice. Was she really so old-fashioned, she wondered in disgust, that she wanted Cormack to buy *her* a similar declaration of intent?

Yes, she did! And what on earth was the point of yearning for the unattainable?

'Where's Simon?' asked Lola.

'Asleep,' answered Cormack. 'I put him down about ten minutes ago.'

Triss saw the assessing look which passed between Lola and Geraint as they jumped to entirely the wrong conclusion. They probably thought that she and Cormack were about to join them for a double wedding, she decided gloomily.

'Oh, I do love Simon!' sighed Lola. 'How I'd love babies of our own! And soon, please, Geraint, darling? Lots and lots of them!'

'I want you to myself for a while before we start having babies, Miss Hennessy!' responded the devastating Welshman, with an almost imperceptible wink at Cormack.

Triss and Cormack left the lovebirds behind. They were driving slowly towards the restaurant when Cormack noticed a man with a long-lens camera hiding not very inconspicuously beneath a tree.

'Look.' He pointed.

'Paparazzi?' queried Triss.

'Looks like it.'

'Wonder why? Is it you?' she wondered aloud, but he shook his head.

'I'm much too boring and low-profile for the tabloids,' he smiled. 'No, it's Dominic. I hate to say I told you so.'

'Well, he shouldn't be so rich and so good-looking,' observed Triss, and Cormack shot her an unfathomable look.

'So he appeals to you, does he?' he queried softly.

'No.'

Oddly, he did not pursue it. In fact, he waited until they were taken to a prime-position table in the restaurant which overlooked the lake before he spoke again.

The other diners watched closely as they sat down, but neither Triss nor Cormack noticed. They were given menus, but the print was a blur to Triss, and she found herself looking rather helplessly across the table at Cormack.

'Two Caesar salads to begin with,' he told the waiter, interpreting her look correctly. 'Then roast salmon with green beans. Half a bottle of Vouvray and some iced water, please.'

He handed their menus back and the two of them sat in silence while the waiter adjusted their cutlery, poured their drinks, then left them.

Triss felt nervous and scared, and then Cormack leaned across the table, picked up her hand from where it lay inertly on the table, and said softly, 'I love you very much, Triss Alexander. So will you please marry me?'

CHAPTER TWELVE

TRISS stared at Cormack disbelievingly. 'You don't,' she told him in a hollow whisper. 'Please don't say you do when you don't.'

He frowned. 'Don't what? Don't want to marry you? Oh, I do, Triss. This is, after all, the second time of asking, remember?'

'But you don't *love* me!' she hissed back angrily, uncaring that people were watching her. 'You're just saying that because you want Simon and you know that I come as part of the package! And you know that I wouldn't dream of marrying you unless I knew that you loved me...'

'Wouldn't you?' he asked interestedly.

She eyed him suspiciously. 'What?'

'Marry me if I *didn't* love you? Be honest now, Triss.'

His blue eyes were piercingly direct, and Triss found that she could not look into them and tell a lie. And hadn't she already decided that afternoon that she *would* marry him, if he still wanted her to?

'Yes,' she admitted in a low voice. 'I think I would.'

'And why would you do that?' he coaxed softly.

Should she risk her pride with an honest answer? Didn't she owe him that much after everything she had done to him? 'Because I have more than enough love to go round,' she told him simply. 'For both of us.'

He started grinning. And grinning. And then he began to chuckle. In all the time she had known him, she had never seen Cormack laugh quite so uninhibitedly.

'What's so funny?' demanded Triss indignantly.

'Nothing. Everything. Oh, darling, you have just made every dream I ever had come true.'

'Cormack—'

But he shook his head. 'Let me just say this, Triss. Let me get it off my chest. When our relationship soured before—'

'It was through my jealousy,' she put in firmly.

'Well, yes—partly. But I couldn't have made you feel very secure if you believed that I was capable of infidelity.'

'I don't think I actually believed *that*,' she admitted. 'I just didn't want beautiful women fawning all over you whenever I wasn't around. *I* wanted to be around you all the time, Cormack, and yet I thought that if I was, then you wouldn't want me any more.'

'But why?' he queried, in a stunned voice. 'Why on earth would you think that?'

'Because I was a successful globe-trotting model—and *that's* the woman you fell in love with! Wouldn't you have felt a little short-changed to discover that suddenly my life's ambition was to be a *hausfrau*?'

'Sweetheart, sweetheart,' he chided softly. 'People change. That's natural—and right. Otherwise no one would settle down and get married and have babies.' He sighed. 'We should have discussed it instead of letting it drive a wedge between us. And that was *my* fault.'

'How?'

'Because of my background, I guess.' He shrugged. 'Growing up with my father...' His voice tailed off, and Triss winced as she remembered the beatings he'd used to endure.

She squeezed his hand and he flashed her the sweetest smile of gratitude.

'It was a tough, working-class area of Belfast,' he continued, though his voice held no trace of bitterness. 'Where men were taught to drink or to punch their woes away. Certainly never to do anything as wimpish as analyse or talk about their feelings! And, though I escaped to the States just as soon as I could, I took that inability to open up and communicate with me.

'Triss, darling.' His voice was very sombre. 'Just look into my eyes and tell me that you don't believe I love you.'

She slowly raised her face to meet his unflinching gaze, and it was as though a curtain had just been lifted, for the love which blazed out from his blue eyes almost blinded her with its intensity.

'I believe you, Cormack.' She blinked, close to tears. 'I believe you.'

He ran a finger in a tiny, sensual circle round the centre of her palm and then looked up, his dark-fringed eyes suddenly serious. 'I've a confession,' he admitted.

But, strangely enough, Triss knew that nothing he could ever tell her now would shock her. Not now. 'Go on.'

'The New Year's Eve party. That fateful night. I knew you were going to be there.'

Somehow it was less surprising than she would have expected it to be. 'How?'

'Martha rang me—'

'*Martha* did?'

'After you'd been to see them. She told me that the two of us needed our heads knocking together— but of course in my stubbornness I refused to believe her. I went there convinced that seeing you again would be enough to banish the spell you had cast on me for ever. But, of course, it had exactly the opposite effect.' He paused. 'Are you angry?'

'With Martha?'

'No. With me.'

'I'm rather flattered that you should have gone chasing across the snowy countryside in order to exorcise my ghost,' she murmured.

'And a fat lot of good it did!' he murmured wryly. 'And now, of course, I'd fly round the world a hundred times just to catch a glimpse of your beautiful face, Triss Alexander. Oh, *hell*!' He briefly buried his face in his hands then looked up at her mock-despairingly. 'Did I really say *that*?'

'Yes, you really did!' she gurgled contentedly. 'And I rather like it when you're being sloppy.'

'Then you'll marry me?'

'Yes,' she whispered.

'When?'

'Tomorrow?'

He gave her a mock frown. 'Don't know if I can wait that long,' he murmured, then eyed the two plates of Caesar salad which the waiter had just placed on the table in front of them. He wrinkled his nose. 'Can you?'

'Are we talking about marriage now?' she queried primly. 'Or bed?'

His eyes glinted. 'Bed.'

'I thought you'd never ask,' Triss sighed, and stood up as Cormack took a wad of notes from his wallet and flung them down on the table without even bothering to count them.

They could barely wait until they were outside before they were in each other's arms and kissing each other like there was no tomorrow.

Inside the restaurant, the two Italian waiters looked on at the embracing couple indulgently, while several of the women sighed jealously and were *almost*—but not quite—tempted to give in to the dessert trolley.

In fact, as one heavily jewelled and bone-thin woman remarked to her equally bone-thin friend, she didn't know why some people *bothered* going out to eat, when food was obviously the last thing on their minds.

And Triss and Cormack—if they could have heard—would have agreed with her wholeheartedly!

* * * * *

HARLEQUIN ✦ PRESENTS®

REVENGE
is Sweet
—*when it leads to love!*

Look out for this irresistible new trilogy
by popular Presents author
Sharon Kendrick:

March 1998:
GETTING EVEN (#1945)

April 1998:
KISS AND TELL (#1951)

May 1998:
SETTLING THE SCORE (#1957)

Three lavish houses, three glamorous couples—
three passionate reasons for revenge....

Available wherever Harlequin books are sold.

Take 4 bestselling love stories FREE

Plus get a FREE surprise gift!

Special Limited-time Offer

Mail to Harlequin Reader Service®

3010 Walden Avenue
P.O. Box 1867
Buffalo, N.Y. 14240-1867

YES! Please send me 4 free Harlequin Presents® novels and my free surprise gift. Then send me 6 brand-new novels every month, which I will receive months before they appear in bookstores. Bill me at the low price of $3.12 each plus 25¢ delivery and applicable sales tax, if any*. That's the complete price and a savings of over 10% off the cover prices—quite a bargain! I understand that accepting the books and gift places me under no obligation ever to buy any books. I can always return a shipment and cancel at any time. Even if I never buy another book from Harlequin, the 4 free books and the surprise gift are mine to keep forever.

106 HEN CE65

Name	(PLEASE PRINT)
Address	Apt. No.
City	State Zip

This offer is limited to one order per household and not valid to present Harlequin Presents® subscribers. *Terms and prices are subject to change without notice. Sales tax applicable in N.Y.

UPRES-696   ©1990 Harlequin Enterprises Limited

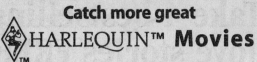